MUSIC HEARD IN HI-FI

Noel Alumit's graceful, understated stories resonate long after one is done reading them. Each one is an engraving of the diasporic Filipino experience, etched with finely drawn emotions of melancholy, longing, regret, and love. Deeply personal, often queer, always vulnerable, these stories reveal the ways in which history embeds itself in the body, in the mind, and, most of all, in the lonely soul.

—Viet Thanh Nguyen, Pulitzer Prize Winner,
The Sympathizer

These achingly tender short stories, centering around Filipino lives in Los Angeles, cross all kinds of borders—gender, nation, opportunity, risk, the moment when life changes direction forever. They will crack your heart wide open.

—Janet Fitch, *White Oleander*,
Chimes of a Lost Cathedral

Noel Alumit's brilliant, long-awaited collection, *Music Heard in Hi-Fi & Other Stories*, spans decades, from the 1960s to the present, and is set mostly in Greater Los Angeles and Manila. Alumit is a storyteller who writes with profound compassion and sharp observations. He dramatizes the highs and lows of people who are not typically centered in movies and books, and trains his attention on the tragedy and beauty that has always been there if only we had paid more attention. A compelling, vibrant collection that you can read in one sitting, but will want to return to again and again.

—Grace Talusan, *The Body Papers*

Surprise is embedded in Noel Alumit's page-turning *Music Heard in Hi-Fi & Other Stories*. The unexpected outs itself with revelatory prose—like secrets tired of being hidden. Noel Alumit's dancing prose touches the reader in surprising ways.

—Dr. Michael Datcher, *Animating Black and Brown Liberation: A Theory of American Literatures*

In *Music Heard in Hi-Fi & Other Stories*, author Noel Alumit introduces an array of characters I don't often get to meet in literature: a transman who longs to be a pallbearer at his father's funeral, a teen who testifies against the man who assaulted him at the beach, a woman who reluctantly relays her story of being imprisoned as an activist in her youth. Each character is poised at the intersection of culture, class, gender identity, and family history, and each resonates as a complex individual I'll still be thinking about for a long time to come.

—Terry Wolverton, author, *Stealing Angel*

Music Heard in Hi-Fi & Other Stories collects eight stories that are pithy and rich and evoke Filipino American life in the Los Angeles area. The stories, which have all been previously published, give the readers a good sense of his characters' histories – in their Philippine homeland as well as their new adopted home in America.

—Cecilia Manguerra Brainard, *When the Rainbow Goddess Wept* and *Growing Up Filipino*

MUSIC HEARD IN HI-FI

& Other Stories

Noel Alumit

REBEL SATORI PRESS
New Orleans & New York

Published in the United States of America by
A Rebel Satori Imprint
www.rebelsatoripress.com

This is a work of fiction. Names, characters, places, and incidents are the product of the author's imagination and are used fictitiously and any resemblance to actual persons, living or dead, business establishments, events, or locales is entirely coincidental. The publisher does not have any control over and does not assume any responsibility for author or third-party websites or their content.

Book design by Sven Davisson
Author Photo by James Pratt

Paperback ISBN: 978-1-60864-278-6
Ebook ISBN: 978-1-60864-279-3

Library of Congress Control Number: 2023938509

Contents

I'm truly grateful to the following publications for giving these stories a place to settle.

The Positive Effects of Yoga, Story Quarterly (2021)
Brandon, McSweeney's (2018)
The Dreams that Made Delya Arraya Cavanaugh Weep, Lodestar Quarterly (2003)
Guest List Girls, Lodestar Quarterly (2005)
Tito Abalez on the Brink of Manhood, Asian Pacific American Journal (2002)
Music Heard in Hi-Fi, Sunday Salon (2015)
A Letter Written at Tommy's Hamburgers, Filipinotown: Voices from Los Angeles (2014)
Laconic Messages of Love, Saints and Sinners (2011);
Best Gay American Short Stories (2012)

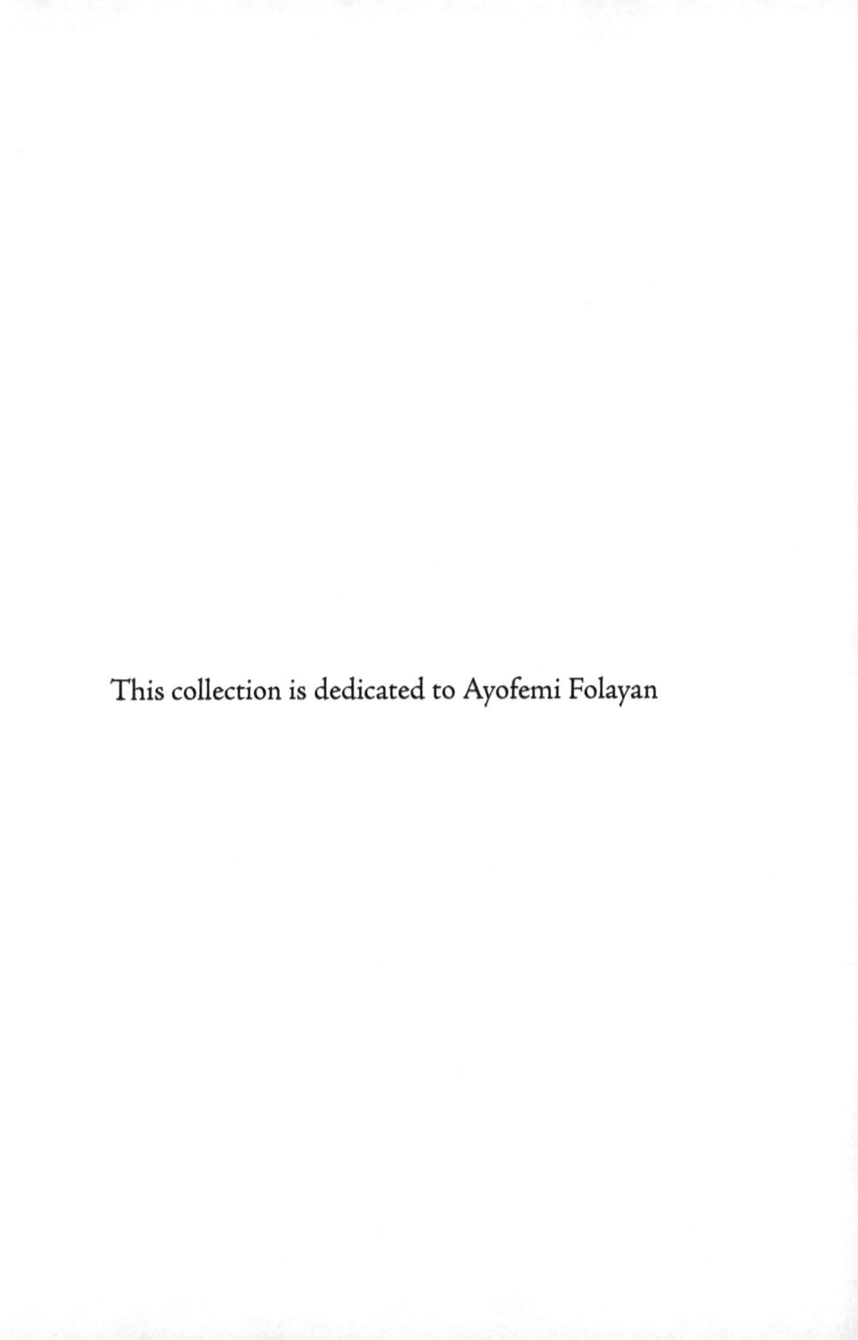

This collection is dedicated to Ayofemi Folayan

Like my grandfather
I collect
the songs of birds.
          Tula, Chris Santiago

Brandon

Brandon Silverio heard the phone ringing. It was the special phone, located in the hallway, meant only for communication to and from the Philippines. He knew it was his mother. Who else would be calling him at three in the morning? He had moved to Los Angeles in 1962, twelve years ago, and since then he'd had to put up with occasional early morning calls from his mom. They were usually calls ordering Brandon to mail some product that wasn't available in the Philippines. ("Send some of that Jean Naté?" his mother said."I think Revlon makes it. An American woman said it was big in the states. Send me some of that!") That was the price for being the only one in his family to move to America—he would have to buy things for them and send them home, he knew.

As the phone rang, Brandon thought of ignoring it. His son, Eric, was a heavy sleeper and could sleep through anything. His wife Jane was not. Jane stirred but he patted her shoulder letting her know that he would get it.

Brandon stumbled out of bed and made his way through the dark hallway.

"*Ano nang yari?*" Brandon said into the receiver.

"Why don't you properly greet a caller? Instead of saying, 'What happened?'"

"Sorry, Mom. Hello. Now, what happened?"

There was a pause, then his mother said, "I have to tell you some bad news."

Brandon leaned against the wall; the phone cradled in his shoulder.

"What's the matter, Mom?"

Brandon heard his mother sobbing, "It's Dad. Heart attack. He died this morning."

He dropped the phone, then reached down to get it. He stayed on the ground, sitting cross legged.

"Come home," she said. "You have to come home."

Home. Brandon looked at the pictures on the wall. There were photos of his new American life with his new American family. Brandon and Jane and Eric. His father would have been proud of the kind of husband and dad he was making.

"Let me see what kind of time I can take off work," Brandon said. "I'll find the next flight back."

Brandon went to his bed, thinking about his father.

"Everything all right, sugar?" Jane said.

"No, my father died. I'm going to have to go home, back to Dagupan."

"Oh, baby, I'm sorry. I know how much you loved him."

Brandon kept photos of family members in their living room. It was fair to say photos of his father were the most prominent.

"Anything I can do?" Jane said.

"No. I'll be all right," he said. He wanted to cry but didn't. He fingered the seams of his pajama pants, clothes he made himself. He knew his father would be proud of the craftsmanship. He sat in bed, wondering how he'd make the trip back homework. He looked at Jane, who had resumed her sleep.

Brandon had met Jane at a concert in Macarthur Park in 1968. Meeting Jane was the best part of that year, one that saw the death of Martin Luther King, Jr. and Robert Kennedy.

Brandon had been with Jane for six years now, took an active part in raising Jane's son, Eric. He almost didn't want to date a woman with a kid, but Jane wore flowers in her hair, the way hippies did back then, and couldn't resist how a daisy petal had fallen onto her face, appearing like a tear under her right eye.

Jane was also Filipino, born and raised in San Francisco. They didn't make Filipino girls like her in the Philippines. Jane said that she was proudly atheist and didn't bother marrying Eric's father, a white man from Sausalito. Jane was a carefree, open-minded woman. That meant a lot to Brandon.

●

Within twenty-four hours Brandon had made arrangements to return to the Philippines. Other Filipino men talked with Brandon, offering memories of the passing of their own fathers.

"You'll be one of the pallbearers then?" one man asked.

"Yeah, sure," Brandon quickly replied.

Jane had packed his suitcase for his trip home. One suitcase belonged to him. Another suitcase was packed with gifts for his family. Brandon packed new Levi jeans that his brothers would love. American gossip magazines for their wives. Stuffed animals and candy for his nephews and nieces. Bath products for his mother. Not even a funeral diminished his role as gift giver from the States.

"All set?" Jane asked.

"Yup," he replied. "Where's Eric?"

"In his room."

Brandon called out to him. "Eric, say good-bye to me."

"Bye," he hollered from down the hall.

"Eric," Brandon called, with a bit of grit in his voice.

A door opened and slammed. Eric showed up with his arms crossed. Brandon looked at the boy who was slowly becoming a man. Eric was 10 and looked like his mother Jane, a wide face with a small mouth. Brandon was grateful. He didn't know if he could look into the face of a boy who resembled his father, an irresponsible lout hitchhiking through Canada.

"Take care of your mom," Brandon said. "You're the man of the house now."

"I'm always the man of the house."

"Eric, please," Jane said.

Brandon looked at Eric and squinted. With that squint, Brandon took away the new skateboard he promised Eric for his birthday, the new camera he wanted for Christmas, and the extra cash he slipped him in addition to the allowance.

"Sorry," Eric said, slumping against the wall. His arms falling to his side.

Brandon detected genuine remorse from the boy. He tousled the youth's hair, letting him know that he was forgiven. He straightened the shirt Eric was wearing, adjusting it so it hung properly.

●

Brandon landed in Manila at two in the morning. He had chosen to land late so his relatives wouldn't greet him en masse. On other visits, he'd landed during the day and a bus load of relatives greeted him at the gate. It was overwhelming. This time it was just his brother Edwin. Brandon knew that Edwin would love the chance to leave Dagupan and spend a few days in Manila.

Edwin was only a few years older than Brandon. Next to his father, Edwin was the second most loved man in Brandon's life. As children, they walked to school together, played together, even slept in the same bed until it became clear one mattress could not sustain two growing bodies.

At school when Brandon got teased for playing sports better than most, Edwin came along to set the other kids straight. Unfortunately, one of those kids was Bing, a distant cousin on their mother's side. Brandon still got chills just thinking of his cousin Bing, a skinny, trouble-making boy who enjoyed sniffing glue.

Brandon always tried to distance himself from Bing. Even as a child, he wanted to know why they let an idiot like Bing come around. Mr. Silverio explained that Bing's family often bought clothes from the shop. During the holidays, Bing's family bought enough dresses and trousers to keep them busy for weeks. For this reason, Bing, despite his ways, would always be treated well around the family.

Brandon smiled when he exited the plane, seeing Edwin standing there. He gave his brother a huge hug. He barely winced when Edwin called him the name that he was born with.

"Brenda," Edwin said, "you're looking well."

"Brandon," he corrected.

"Ay, sorry. It's hard to change."

"Tell me about it."

They went to a bar near Manila Bay. Brandon raised a San Miguel beer to his lips

then asked, "How's Mama?"

"The same. Dramatic. Ordering everyone here and there."

"Sounds like the woman hasn't changed."

"No, but you have. Your hair, clothes…Mom is not going to be too happy."

"Don't worry. I'm prepared."

"Are you sure, Brenda? Sorry, Brandon."

"That's okay. Call me Brenda. I might as well get used to it."

In the morning, Brandon woke up in his hotel, ready to take the five-hour drive to his hometown. That was another reason he wanted to arrive in Manila late at night. He'd have time to adjust to his new surroundings before taking that long bus ride home.

Brandon got up from his bed and pulled out the luggage. It was filled with his old clothes: blouses, some pants, a few skirts, and pumps. They were the same clothes he brought back to the Philippines every time he visited. He sighed at the sight of them. Maybe the garments were a little outdated, but they would do. After twelve years, he could still fit into them. He supposed he should be proud of that, but he wasn't.

Once Edwin exited the bathroom, Brandon entered and dressed. He was thankful that he had small breasts, but they were breasts none the less. In America, he did everything he could to hide them: bind them, slouch, and wear those billowy barongs. He didn't put the pomade in his hair. He let it fall across his face. Before leaving he had taken some of Jane's cosmetics. He applied a little bit of lipstick, a little bit of mascara. His hand shook as he brushed his lashes but knew that his mother would lay into him if he didn't apply at least an ounce of make-up.

With the exception of Edwin, no one in his family knew about the life he led in America. Brandon squirted a bit of lotion into his hand. It was coco butter. To Brandon it was the most feminine of scents. He looked into the mirror and put some earrings on. He smiled and saw a tinge of sadness in his face.

●

Brenda Silverio was the last of six children, born in a small town outside of Dagupan City, Pangasinan Province in the Philippines. She was the only girl and the biggest hope for her mother, Miss Pangasinan, 1939. As soon as she was able to walk Brenda was adorned with a paper crown and sash. Brenda held the crown long enough for a photo to be taken, then immediately ripped off her sash and crumpled her crown. She was two years old.

Mrs. Silverio laughed, thinking the child to be precocious. No one knew that would be the beginning of the girl's rejection of anything considered overtly feminine or garishly frilly.

It took, under the direction of Mrs. Silverio, the strength of three maids to prevent young Brenda from running out with her brothers to play ball. By the time she was ten, no army could hold Brenda down. She burst from her home with a fury to race her brothers to school, staying late into the afternoon, under the burning sun, to run, to swim, to jump, to tumble.

When she arrived home, her mother screamed at her for

returning darkened and sweaty.

"Brenda, you will never be Miss Philippines if you keep acting like that," she said.

Matters became worse when cousin Bing had no problem telling Mrs. Silverio how Brenda often behaved at school.

"She fights the boys, Auntie," Bing said. "She picks fights with them for no reason."

"They pick on me," Brenda cried, swinging a fist at Bing.

Mrs. Silverio slapped her daughter for being so violent, then pulled Bing close to her.

"Oh, Auntie," Bing said, "what perfume are you wearing? You smell like flowers."

"Oh, just something I used to wear during my pageant days."

"You are still the most beautiful woman in the province."

Brenda wanted to vomit at the sight of her mother hugging this wretched boy.

To her father Ernesto Silverio, Brenda could do no wrong. When she was small, he recognized the girl as a headstrong creature with a spirit for adventure. She'd throw on his old suits and stumble around in his loafers, acting like a big shot. The site of this little girl wearing his clothes made Mr. Silverio bend over with laughter, then pick her up and swing her in the air.

Brenda preferred hanging out with her father in the tailoring shop than cooking at home. She loved seeing the men come into the store, try on various coats and hats. Her father would measure, mark, and pin clothes on some of the most distinguished men in town.

There wasn't a wedding, a graduation, a funeral that his father didn't know about. He dressed men the way he wanted to be dressed: with complete dignity, style, and practicality. Mr. Silverio showed up for work in a suit that he made himself, knowing that he was his best advertisement. He wore suits of emerald green or sea blue or cloud white, mostly in linens appropriate for the tropical weather.

Brenda's favorite suit was the one Mr. Silverio wore when someone truly important came into the shop, like the governor. It was a gray sharkskin that Brenda thought her father looked best in. The fabric had been delivered from Hong Kong and it was easily the most expensive suit Mr. Silverio had ever made for himself.

Allowing her to work in her father's shop was the only concession her mother made. Brenda learned how to operate a sewing machine, which fit into Mrs. Silverio's idea of femininity. Her brothers knew how to operate a sewing machine also, but Brenda really took to it. By the time, she was thirteen, she was the one sewing the best suits for the finest men.

By the time she was sixteen, Brenda was sure that her life would not be in that town. She preferred pants to dresses and tried to wear them as much as she could. Mrs. Silverio wouldn't have it. When Mrs. Silverio made Brenda wear a hideous white dress and veil to a Mass, Brenda couldn't stomach it anymore.

Somehow her father knew this. Mr. Silverio had encouraged his sons to stay, help with the family business, but he encouraged Brenda to leave.

"Go," he said, "go to Manila. You might be happy there."

Brenda almost cried. She took it as permission to truly be himself. One year she returned home and sat with her father. Brenda's long hair had been shortened to her shoulders. "I'm going to move to the States," she said. She remembered her father's long pause.

"What will you find in America?"

"I don't know," she said. "But I won't find anything here."

Again, he said, "Go." He extended his hand, his knuckles facing her, a major sign of his blessing. Brenda got down on her knees and lowered her forehead to meet his hand. She filed paperwork to go to America the next day.

●

The bus ride back to her town was long. Her brother Edwin sat by her side. The bus pulled into the main square of town. She exited the bus, and the smell of her former life came rushing back to her. The food from local vendors made her smile. She saw the big church where all the passages of life happened, from christening to funeral. She held her bag close to her when a thin, jittery man approached and gave her a hug.

"Brenda, welcome back," the man said.

Brenda pulled away. It was Bing. He took her bag and led them to a car.

"I'll drive. I like to drive," Bing said.

Brenda sat in the back watching Bing's head bounce to music on the radio. The road they drove on was a dusty and lonely one. A few times they swerved. Brenda knew that his cousin was intoxicated.

"In America they're starting to take driving drunk seriously. You can go to jail," Brenda said.

"Thank goodness we're in the Philippines," Bing said with a snort.

Asshole, Brenda thought.

The Silverio home was part of a compound: several houses clustered together to let others know that this was not just a family, but a series of families who looked out for each other. They had all been tied together by marriages or births. Ask anyone living there and they could count back at least four generations how each family member was related.

The compound occupied six acres of land, a half a mile from the beach. It was a green, lush area with colorful flowers dotting the grounds. All of the homes had furniture made locally. Indeed, Dagupan City was known for its woodwork.

Mrs. Silverio stood at the opening of the compound, her arms outstretched. Brenda embraced the old woman and gave her a kiss on the cheek.

"America has been good to you," Mrs. Silverio said. "You don't seem to be starving. You've gotten fat."

Brenda sighed. "Actually, mom, I weigh the same from when I left."

"Oh, Auntie," Bing said. "Even under difficult circumstances, you still manage to remain beautiful."

"Thank you, Bing," Mrs. Silverio said. "You always know what to say."

Brenda rolled her eyes.

"Let's see your father," Mrs. Silverio said, walking her through the crowded house. A wave of relatives hugged and kissed her. Brenda returned their affections. She was truly grateful to see them. She was led to the middle of the room, where her father rested in a mahogany casket.

It took less than a second for Brenda to fall to her knees sobbing. No one saw the slight smile on Mrs. Silverio's face, who approved of her daughter's fine display of grief.

●

Away from the main house, where Mrs. Silverio wanted to stay with the guests, Edwin brought Brenda to his house where she unloaded her American gifts on her family. Her brothers (in addition to Edwin, there were Marco, Ryan, Joel, and Cesar) graciously accepted the new jeans. Their wives (Grace, Erlinda, Nina, Marites, and Joanne) planted kisses on Brenda's face upon receiving the lotions and perfumes.

They ate rich meats topped with garlic rice and desserts of sweet beans and fruits. They caught up on neighborhood gossip and sang songs they used to hear on the radio. San Miguel was brought out and the memories of their father followed.

"I messed up on a suit," said Joel. "One pant leg was longer than the other. Dad, cut it up and fixed it like that. The customer even gave a generous tip."

Cesar chimed in, "At school, people gave me respect because they knew Dad was a good man."

"He was the first one to welcome me to the family," said Grace. "I felt like I was his daughter immediately!"

"Me, too," said Joanne. "Your father was always so kind. Your mother on the other hand…"

They all burst out with a knowing laugh.

"I felt like he just wanted us to be happy," Edwin said. "Isn't that right, Brenda?"

"Yes, that's true," Brenda agreed.

There was a very long pause, so long Brenda knew that it was meant for her.

"He wanted you to be happy, too," said Marco.

"I know," Brenda said.

"Is there anyone in the states you're seeing?" asked Marites.

Brenda remained silent. She looked to the ground and nodded slightly.

Marites continued, "Do you want to tell us?"

Brenda looked up and saw the faces of her family. Her father raised good fine sons; in turn they chose fine wives. She wiped the lipstick from her face and said, "I met this girl in 1968…"

●

Brenda walked about the house. Her shoulders slumped over. Her head bowed. Her father was gone. The concept was settling in her bones, and, with that understanding, the weight of who she was disappeared. Empty. Cold. Lifeless. She looked into the mirror and saw the fabric of her pajamas on her body. Who is that? She wondered. All she saw was a scarecrow: clothes on some propped-up creature, void of feeling and purpose.

She heard her mother talking, a faint determined voice at the kitchen table. Brenda walked toward the sound and found her mother with a notepad in front of her.

"Make sure there's enough food," Mrs. Silverio said. She was talking to the maids, preparing for the funeral gathering. "I don't want to hear about how people left hungry. Is that clear?"

"Mom, what can I do to help?"

"Brenda, I need for you to tell people about Dad's passing. Make sure everyone knows."

"Of course."

"We need to gather and let people know their duties. All of your five brothers will be needed. They'll carry the casket. We need one more pall bearer."

Brenda looked down at the floor, then said, "I'll do it."

"What? No. The casket will be heavy. We need a man to do it."

"Mom, if my five other brothers will be there, I can hold up my end."

"Brenda, only men are pall bearers."

"Mom, this is the 1970's. It's a different world. I want to help carry Dad's body."

"Nonsense."

"I want to do it."

"Your cousin Bing will do it."

"Bing? He's not good enough to wash Dad's shoes, let alone lift his body."

"Why are you always so hard on him?"

"Mom, there are a million men who should be a pall bearer over Bing. We can find somebody else."

Her mother didn't respond.

"Why Bing?"

"Funerals are expensive…"

Brenda clenched her fists. Bing's parents are helping pay for the funeral. Brenda wished she had the money to chip in. She thought of the music lessons, baseball uniforms, the Christmas gifts she gave to her son in the states. She didn't regret it for a minute, but it meant she didn't have money for unplanned expenses, like a funeral. She left the house to think.

●

She knocked on the door and heard scuffling. A prostitute opened the door. There was one whore house in town and Brenda knew she'd find Bing there. The prostitute was young, maybe fourteen.

"Yes?" said the girl.

"I know Bing's here. Where is he?"

"Let her in," a voice said.

Brenda entered and saw her half naked cousin on the bed. He was skinny, really skinny. He didn't seem to have an ounce of muscle on him.

"Get out of here," Bing said to the whore. The girl obliged.

"I want to talk to you," said Brenda, taking a seat on a wooden chair by the wall.

"I figured that. If you come into this place, you must want to talk to me pretty bad."

"It's about my father. I want to carry him into the ground."

"That is reserved for the men of the family."

Exactly, Brenda thought, and you don't even come close. She said, "Bing, it would mean a lot to me if I could help carry the casket."

"It would mean a lot to me to carry the casket, too. Your father was always good to me. Unlike you."

"We may not have gotten along in the past, but now is not the time to go into that. I'm asking if I could take your place as one of my father's pallbearers."

"I might consider it…if you beg."

"What?"

"You always thought you were better than me. You love your father? Beg me to take my place. If you get on your knees and beg, I'd be more than willing to give up my spot."

"If I beg, you'd let me be a pallbearer for my father?" Brenda sat there for a long while. "My father didn't raise me to beg for anything." She got up, picked up the wooden chair she was sitting on and threw it at Bing, then sauntered out the door. She heard cursing as she walked out.

●

"Brenda," Edwin said, "I know you feel obligated to do this, but I'm not going to give this up."

She decided to approach her brothers to see if they'd be willing to give up their spot beside the casket. Predictably, each one sympathized but ultimately said, no. She was dejected.

"We're packing up some of Dad's clothes," Edwin said, "See if there is something of his that you might want to keep."

Brenda went through the box of clothing. She went through the garments carefully, smelling the musk of her father and the mildew of time. She saw his old T-shirts and slacks, thin dress socks, and leather belts. The denim jeans and short-sleeve oxfords.

Brenda sat there and remembered sitting on her father's lap and pulling at the collar of some of these shirts when she was a child.

She found another box, carefully packed. She examined it and smiled. This was filled with his old suits, thin lapel coats and narrow legged pants. Linen garments with a bit of wrinkle. Khaki's that still maintained a crease on the leg. Brenda lowered her head, bringing the clothes to her face, inhaling them deeply. She reached the bottom of the box and her eyes widened. It was the gray shark skin suit—her father's favorite. She put on the coat and yes, it was too big. She didn't bother trying on the trousers. She could tell that they were way too large for her.

She folded the clothes, as if handling a small child. She cradled it in her arms and left the room.

●

Brandon opened the door of the church. His hair was slicked back and his face free of make-up. He walked down the aisle of the church, preparing to sit by his family. His father's casket in the center of it all. He wore an altered suit, the gray shark skin that belonged to his dad. He was up all night refitting the garments to match his body. He heard whispers as he walked through the crowd.

It wasn't until he joined his family in the front pew that someone said in a very loud whisper, "Is that Brenda?"

Brandon felt the stares of his siblings and the intense fury of his mother, but being in front of God, wearing threads that his father once wore, Brandon felt the handsomest he'd ever felt. His shoulders were back, his hands folded in front of him. He followed the rituals of the Mass, waiting for the moment the casket would be led down the aisle, out the doors of the church, and through the hundred yards to the cemetery.

"Would anyone like to come up and say something about our departed Ernesto Silverio?" the priest offered.

There was a brief moment of silence, then one by one members of the audience got up to share a fond memory or two of Mr. Silverio. Each one of Brandon's brothers shared memories of his boyhood with their father. Mrs. Silverio dabbed tears from her eyes. Brandon could feel his mother's fury abate with each person who spoke sweet words of Ernesto Silverio.

Brandon looked around and saw that cousin Bing was at the far end of the pew, dozing off. From his moments of nervous twitters, Brandon knew the asshole was loaded.

The bastard's high at my father's funeral, Brandon thought.

"Is there anyone else who'd like to speak?" asked the priest.

Brandon got up and approached the podium. "I'd…I'd like to say that I was raised by the best man in the world. If…If I could be half the man he was, I'd be satisfied."

After the final prayer, the priest asked the pallbearers to arrange themselves around the casket. The men lifted the coffin and proceeded down the aisle. They all had calm expressions, except for Bing who was sweating, wiping his forehead with his coat sleeve. Bing tripped and the coffin heaved forward with an audible gasp heard from the mourners.

Brandon walked behind the pallbearers, his mother a few feet away, silently weeping. She seemed to forget that her daughter was now a son. Despite what differences they may have had, they both loved the same man. When she appeared too grief stricken to walk, Brandon scurried beside her and touched her elbow, letting her know he was there for her.

The church doors opened, and the six men walked down the several steps of the church. Bing lost his balance and fell, and his end of the casket sank, causing the other five men to stop briefly and collect themselves. Bing began to chuckle, and it became clear to everyone that he was drunk.

Bing tried to stand, but Brandon stepped forward. He firmly put his hand on Bing's shoulder, guiding him away and depositing him into the crowd. Brandon took hold of the casket. It was heavy, but he knew he could carry his end.

The Dreams that Made Delya Arraya-Cavanaugh Weep

She awoke with a film of sweat on her forehead. She thought of waking Baker and telling him about it, but after 18 years of marriage, she knew what he would say: "Did you have one of your nightmares again?" She could never consider her dreams about Franky a nightmare.

Mahal kita, Franky would say in the flimsy reality of sleep. *Mahal Kita.*

She hadn't dreamed of her youth in The Philippines in awhile. Sometimes she didn't dream of that period for weeks, months, years at a time. Then like scurrying rats, they came: the dreams that inundated her. Dreams that carried themselves into her days. She would imagine seeing him late in the afternoons when shadows were most present, shifting the contours of a stranger's face to look like Franky. Once she saw him crossing Wilshire Blvd or entering Macy's department store. These dreams made her drive to Santa Monica Beach, walk over the sea and weep.

Delya put on her robe, walked downstairs to the kitchen, and looked through the window. She waited for that thin shock of light to creep over the earth. Soon Baker would be up, Marta and Sam would be arguing about who would be the one to drive to school, she would eventually be stuck in traffic on the Hollywood Freeway, and she would have to meet this Noah—or was it Neal?—and tell him what she knew.

Mahal kita, Franky said in her dream, as he said in every dream. *Mahal kita.* English translation: I Love You.

●

She stepped out of the shower and blow-dried her hair. She cursed herself for letting her hairdresser talk her into this perm, her shoulder length hair cut and burned into ringlets below her ears. He said it would help her look younger. She secretly hoped some new curls here and there would remove the lines and wrinkles on her face, also perhaps make her tummy disappear, her thighs more firm. What was I thinking? she wondered.

She reminded herself that she had granted the writer only twenty minutes. She would have granted more time if she liked this Noah, but she didn't. She got the impression that he was a spoiled Filipino American, someone who claimed to be proud of his Filipino heritage but had never visited the Philippines.

"Is this Delya?" she remembered him asking on the phone.

"Yes. Speaking."

"Hi, my name is Noah Balagtas." He said his last name slowly and deliberately. Delya knew why he did this; she knew it well: he wanted to let her know that he wasn't just anybody off the street, he came from a particular kind of family, a family Delya was *supposed* to know about. Her job in Senator Bailey's office was to be a liaison to the Asian community. The senator's district had a huge Asian constituency. Indeed, she had heard of this Noah's family name, but she didn't know why. The thought of this kid, who certainly

21

sounded younger than she, asking to speak with Delya, not Mrs. Arraya-Cavanaugh, not *Ginang* Arraya, but Delya. This implied a familiarity that annoyed her.

"I was referred to you," he said, "by Tita Amorez." Tita, yes, a good friend, a friendship that went back twenty-five years. "Tita said you might be able to help me."

"I'll try."

"I'm working on a novel or a book of fiction."

I know what a novel is, stupid, Delya thought. Delya knew she spoke with an accent. For some, an accent immediately made her dumb. She chose to be pleasant. "That's wonderful. How may I help?"

"I'm curious about life under the Marcos regime in the Philippines during the 1970s," he said. "Would I be able to speak to you?" She was silent. "If I may have just a few minutes of your time...." She finally told him, "Twenty minutes. I'm very busy."

"Awesome. I'll put it in my date book. Monday, around nine. Interview with Delya Cavanaugh."

"Delya *Arraya*-Cavanaugh," she said, then hung up. She wanted him to know that she came from a prominent family, too.

●

She got on the freeway wondering how much she should reveal in the interview. Would she speak from the very beginning? Would she tell him she grew up in the suburbs of Manila, went to private Catholic schools? Or should she skip to Franky? Yes. She would do that: talk about Franky. That's why Noah--maybe it was

Nathan--called.

She would tell him that they met in college at the University of the Philippines in Manila. She would tell of Franky's arrogance, his boldness. She would tell of Franky's bushy black hair that hovered over his head like rain clouds. She would tell of how Franky approached her and called her "ma'am."

"How are you today, ma'am? My name is Franky Benitez, and we are having a meeting tonight." He handed her a flyer. She took it.

"My name is Delya Arraya." She saw Franky's eyes narrow. She knew that look, and she nodded to confirm his suspicions, as if to say, Yes, Delya Arraya of Arraya Sugar Company.

"Come to our meeting," he said and indicated the flyer in her hand.

"I'll try," she responded, then walked away, turning back occasionally to look at this boy, whose skin was the color of cinnamon. She watched him watching her. Yes, she would tell of their first meeting, and how that flyer changed her life. It urged of revolution against the President.

What she wouldn't tell him--this Noah or Ned or whatever his name was--was about their second meeting by the fountain, or their third, walking along Roxas Boulevard, or their fourth, watching the waves in Manila Bay.

She wouldn't tell him of being a teenager with a lineless face and falling in love with a man she would spend the rest of her life trying to escape, to forget. She wouldn't tell him how her parents disapproved of her dating him.

Later, her parents screamed at her for getting engaged. She certainly wouldn't tell him that they were lovers. She wouldn't tell

Noah or Ned that Franky said, "I love you" when he orgasmed. Afterwards, he would ask, "Do you love me, too?" He sounded like a child needing reassurance. "Of course, stupid," she said. No, she wouldn't talk of that.

She would, however, tell of how she left Franky for a weekend, rushing to spend time with her parents in the northern city of Baguio, furiously packing, only kissing him briefly as she exited his small apartment. When she returned, Franky was gone. She asked his neighbors if they had seen him. They shook their heads. She went to Rico's, his favorite bar, to St. Augustin's, the church where he prayed, Mama Ginger, the restaurant where he ate most of his dinners. No one knew where he was. Finally, she asked a bartender in Tondo if he'd seen Franky. He told her Franky had gone to visit some friends in Quiapo, a neighborhood in Manila. She was relieved. But when he did not return a week later, she worried.

She had heard of the police taking students away, students who made noise about the President. At some of the rallies she attended with Franky, she'd heard firsthand accounts of what was done to prisoners—the tortures, the beatings, the rapes, the random executions when the jails got too full. She was also told how to find missing persons: ask questions, talk to people. She, along with a bunch of other friends, went to Quiapo asking residents if they had seen Franky. Most said, No. Others said he was picked up with a bunch of other students. She continued to ask people, enlisting the help of other allies. She continued asking late into the night. When her friends became tired and hungry, she went by herself, knocking on doors. It was close to midnight when a dark car drove up next to her, men jumped out and nabbed her. She tried to scream but the plastic bag forced over her head prevented her.

●

The walls of her office have framed degrees and photos of her family and friends. There's a certificate of appreciation from the Mayor of Los Angeles for all of her hard work and a print of a Picasso painting. She pulled out a box of cookies from a file cabinet. She delighted in Pepperidge Farm, particularly their chocolate chip. She looked into the boardroom. This is where she would have the interview, she decided. No one else had plans for it and she liked the big blond wooden table in the middle. The table would keep her a comfortable distance from Noah.

At 8:15, she peered through the curtains hoping he would come earlier. This would mean she could end it sooner. Maybe get some work done. She hadn't been able to concentrate. She had a meeting later in the day to discuss plans for a new recreational center near Echo Park. She would smile and tell people that they had the full support of the senator in creating a new facility for the neighborhood youth to play. She was there to assuage activists who petitioned to get more funding to build parks. She had met activists in her work, men and women who waved signs and made grand speeches, referring to civil rights or cancer or AIDS or discrimination. She'd inform the senator of their concerns. She would translate the angry rhetoric of the activists into a brief, sound bite for the senator to digest. ("They are concerned that Parks and Recreations money will be gutted. They want your assurance that it won't.")

She knew the importance of activism, but sometimes she looked into the faces of these activists and questioned their fervor. It seemed people in America had a lax approach to their social causes, only marching or protesting when they had time. Marches and protests were scheduled only after work or on weekends, and only if the weather was good. Some marchers were even willing to get arrested, but what relief in knowing they would be out in twenty-four hours.

She wondered how many of these so-called activists would put it all on the line. How many people fighting for civil rights this and discrimination that, breast cancer this and AIDS that would risk all of it—their freedom, their family, their livelihood, their comfortable bed, their warm meals, their television—everything they had for their cause?

She wondered when she was arrested if all she and Franky were fighting for--judicial fairness, social reform, freedom of speech, freedom of expression--was worth it. Would she stand firm? Would she crumble? She thought this in a dirty room on the outskirts of Manila. She was placed in a "safehouse." Despite its name, a safehouse was nothing but. Five guards made her sit in a chair and asked for her name. "My name," she said, "is Delya Daluz Montenya Espiritu Arraya." She said her full name slowly and deliberately to let her captors know that she did not come from one prominent family, but four.

They wanted her to sign a document stating her illegal activities, confessing to being a communist, admitting to other crimes she did not commit. If she signed, she was told she would be released. Then again, if she signed, they could keep her. Her signature proof of subversive activity.

She told them she wouldn't sign anything. She told them she didn't do anything wrong. She told them she would hire a lawyer and fight her arrest. She spoke in English to let them know that she was educated, to let them know that she would be missed, to let them know that she wasn't some poor little girl from a small town that would simply go away. She wanted to let these men know, despite their uniforms and their guns, they would not intimidate her. For a split second, she thought about Franky, because he was not wealthy and probably came from the same stock as her captors. This made her sad. She hoped the guards did not see her sadness. She hoped they did not see how she was scared, scared that Franky was hurt somewhere. She was well connected. Franky was not.

She was brave, refusing to cry and fall apart. She would not tell them she was only a teenage girl looking for her boyfriend; she wanted to beg for mercy and be delivered to the front steps of her parents' home. She wanted to go back to school. She wanted all of these things but knew she couldn't go back.

The best her high-profile family could do was to get her into a minimum-security prison instead of a maximum-security cell. She had heard of "maximum security." Prisoners were no longer human there. She could be shut away in a dark room for months at a time or be electrocuted with wires attached to her private parts or gang raped.

In minimum security, she was fed scraps, spoiled fish, and rotted fruit. She endured dysentery. She was forced to see her fellow inmates--students, doctors, teachers, artists, philosophers, nuns--disintegrate into broken men and women, some of whom went insane.

Random executions occurred when the prisons got too full. Men were pulled from their barracks and shot. It was at this time that she began to dream of Franky. She knew what they did to prisoners, and if it weren't for her family name and background, she would have been one of the many who disappeared. She didn't know what happened to Franky, and in not knowing she was forced to imagine, to dream the most heinous tortures committed against him. Did they stab him, then cut him up into little pieces, his remains in an unmarked grave? Did they shoot him in the back of the head, forcing his skull to explode? Did they bend him backward with rope tied from his feet to his neck, causing him to choke himself? Did they disembowel him? She didn't know.

She stayed in prison for two years. It took that long for her lawyer to get the charges against her dismissed.

●

Delya looked out her second-floor window and saw a young man, the writer, park his car, a sports utility vehicle of some kind. She heard the chirp of his car alarm as he locked his door. He wore a green sweater around his neck. She dreaded spending the next twenty minutes with a man who wore his sweater around his neck. She had met men and women like that when her parents sent her to the states to start anew. When she was sent to UCLA to gain her master's in public policy, she went willingly. After two years in prison and the hope of finding Franky finally gone, she wanted to leave. In college, she met a man she loved—loved enough—had two beautiful children and moved into a cottage-style home in the valley. She continued her work in humanitarian efforts, but nothing like she had endured in the Philippines.

She went downstairs to greet him. "Hi," he said, "I'm Noah Balagtas." His name was Noah after all, Delya thought.

"Hello," she said, guiding him to the second-floor boardroom. "Would you like some coffee?"

"Tea, please."

Oh, yes, she thought, it was more fashionable to drink tea these days. She handed him a saucer of cookies, a cup of hot water, and a tea bag. She noted how he was disappointed at having been served Lipton. What did he want? Chamomile in a strainer?

"Thank you for meeting with me. I'm truly grateful," he said. Self-effacing--good, but Delya couldn't quite buy it. There was something disingenuous about him, something that made her uncomfortable. She knew he'd just stepped out of the shower; his face wasn't oily yet. His hair was tousled, the way young people wear their hair these days. All of those expensive cosmetic products to have your hair look like you just got out of bed. He was too clean, too clean to be writing a book about this topic. She also knew he was vain. She noticed how he looked into every window that gave him a reflection.

"Did you have trouble finding the place?" she asked. "No," he said, "I ran the LA marathon, and we ran down this street, past this building." What a joy it must be, she thought, to have the privilege of putting your body through such pain, and pay money for the opportunity. "I run a lot," he said. "I ran a 10K to raise money for breast cancer research. I wanted to do my part. I think I'm gonna run for multiple sclerosis next." Delya wanted to hit him. She had spent two years in prison so future Filipinos could have better lives. And this young man runs occasionally for a good cause.

She watched him pick up a cookie, bite it and put it back on the saucer. He wiped his lips with his finger, the one closest to the pinkie, and she knew immediately that he was gay. She felt more at ease. Gay men did not seem as threatening. Indeed there were gay men, mostly artists, whom she had met in prison.

He pulled out a tape recorder and fiddled with it. "Testing. This is Noah. Interview on March 2." He was nervous, and she relaxed some more. She watched him rewind the tape and listen. It worked. He placed the recorder between them and said, "Anything you can tell me would be helpful. My novel is about a boy whose parents were abducted. They disappeared. I went to Amnesty International to research disappearances under Marcos. I'm amazed that thousands of people simply vanished." Delya was impressed. He'd done his homework.

"Were you born here?" Delya asked.

"Yes."

"Why did your parents come here?"

"Um, to live a better life, I suppose. Though I visited the Philippines a few years back. It was gorgeous. I didn't want to leave. Everything was so cheap."

"People don't leave a country if their lives are good. They leave because their lives are difficult. When did your family arrive?"

"Sometime in the seventies."

The height of the Marcos regime, she knew. People left the Philippines in droves due to economic hardships. The Philippine economy has never recovered from such plundering. Filipinos left to give birth to American children whose primary purpose is to make sure their hair was fashionably messy.

"Why do you want to write this book? Why do you want to talk to me?"

She saw him look up, startled. He sat back in his chair. He took a deep breath

and said, "Because my parents don't want to talk about it. And I'm curious why."

Delya clasped her hands, narrowed her focus onto the tape recorder and said, "I was a student. I met a boy." She told him all that she knew. She didn't mean to, but when she began, she couldn't stop. The twenty-minute interview turned into ninety. She watched the writer's smiling face slowly darken, realizing his little novel--his book of fiction--was more complex than he'd ever intended.

"That's what happened," she said.

He adjusted that damned sweater around his neck. He was uncomfortable, she knew. He reached for his cup of Lipton tea. The cup trembled in his hand as he brought it to his lips.

"Thank you," he croaked.

He was preparing to leave. The interview was over, but not for her. She felt she didn't tell the story quite right. She thought she was too factual, not emotional enough. She didn't convey all that she was feeling. She didn't know how to tell him that she still loved Franky. After twenty years and a whole ocean apart, she still couldn't forget him. Sometimes it got so bad, she felt she could trade in her husband and marriage of 18 years, her two beautiful children, her degree that added extra letters to her name, her job with great benefits to know one thing: What. Happened. To. Franky? How could she convey that she missed the very first man inside her, that she missed the man she kept locked in her dreams to whisper, I love you. How could she say this? She looked down at her hands, and finally said in a whisper more delicate than a spider's web, "I still dream...about him."

She watched Noah out of the periphery of her vision. She learned this skill in prison. She watched him pause, look at her, then look away. He didn't get it, but she hoped that someday he would. Someday, he would listen to the tape, listen to it over and over and understand what she was trying to say.

●

Delya drove to Santa Monica beach, parked her car, and stood at the edge of America. She made her way to the pier, walked on the wooden slats, watching the sea beneath her rise and transform into a deep green. She was standing over the ocean. She closed her eyes and recalled her dream: She held him, unaware of the blood dripping from the puncture holes in his skin. Knife wounds, this time, it was knife wounds. His black hair blended into the dark sky, stars hovered above him, the moon off to the side. Looking up at him, Delya couldn't tell where Franky ended and the universe began.

The Positive Effects of Yoga

After every yoga class, I get an erection. I used to think I got turned on by all the women bending over or arching their backs. When I do yoga at home, just a few sun salutations to start my day, I also get aroused.

I started yoga on advice of my doctor. After decades of regularly playing sports, at 43 my body began to show its wear; my joints and muscles hurt. It didn't hurt in the way that muscles hurt after a good workout. It hurt like there was a strain. It felt like my body was caving in on itself.

My doctor suggested I lay off the running, the basketball, the weightlifting and do activities that caused less stress to my body. I used to do a lot of those activities with my kids, but my wife and I are still trying to figure out a way to schedule visits with our young ones.

At first, I was against doing yoga. I didn't know anyone who did yoga, except women. The guys I knew who did yoga were into astrology or didn't eat meat. There's nothing wrong with that, but that's not me.

Peter, you don't have to do yoga forever, my doctor said, just for a few months to let your body rebuild itself.

I'd been going to a yoga studio on Sunset Boulevard for six weeks now. I'm surprised at how much I actually enjoy it. There's lots of stretching and stillness, things I like. There's an emphasis on balance, which I have trouble with, but I could feel my body getting stronger.

I don't get into crazy positions the way some people do in class. I don't feel the need. If I can't get into some weird pose, like sticking my head under my crotch, I don't do it. Whenever I play sports with other guys, my competitive edge kicks in and I feel like I've got to make the shot, outrun the next guy. In yoga, I don't feel the need to compete, maybe because we start each class meditating. We just sit there and breathe, enjoy the silence. I can't remember the last time I heard silence.

There is one thing I'd like to be able to do in yoga though: a headstand. Even in the beginning classes, we're asked to do headstands. With our fingers clasped behind our heads and our forearms to help support us, we're supposed to hoist our bodies into the air, the tip of our cranium experiencing all that mass. Most people can do a headstand with the wall supporting their bodies. Some can do it without pressing against the wall. I can't do it at all. It feels like I'll crash right through the floor, the crown of my head crushed by the weight of my body. If I can do a headstand, I know I'd accomplish something.

●

On Sunday, I usually worship. I'd be at St. Genevieve's in Panorama City, in the San Fernando Valley, with my family. I like St. Genevieve's, because there are other Filipino families who go there. Since my wife decided she didn't love me anymore, she took the kids and left. Rather, she stayed with the kids and the house and I was asked to leave. Now, I live in a single in Silverlake. On Sunday, I go to yoga instead of Mass.

Another aspect of yoga is that I feel the need to eat better. I buy food at the farmers market in the neighborhood. I think I'm in good shape, women at work say I'm a good-looking man. I'm still aware of my midsection with a bit of my stomach hanging over my belt.

I bought some organic tomatoes. They're supposed to be good for you. I don't know the difference between organic and regular tomatoes, but I buy them anyway. I was reaching for some broccoli when someone said, Don't you go to Urth Yoga on Sunset?

I looked up and saw an Asian woman, mid-thirties, with hair in a ponytail. She wore a maroon jumpsuit and a yoga mat was under her arm.

Yeah, I said. I didn't recognize her at first but I soon realized that she regularly goes to the evening classes. I don't notice a lot of people in class and try to stay away from the women. I tried talking to some of the girls in yoga, but they keep conversation short. I know there are guys who go to yoga to pick up on girls. Maybe they think I'm one of them. I'd tell them in a heartbeat that I'm in love with a woman who doesn't love me anymore.

Yeah, I said. I just started going to Urth a little while ago. Still feel kinda awkward doing it.

Don't be ridiculous, she said. You're more flexible than most guys I know. I smiled and introduced myself, Name's Peter Dantes.

Gia Wong Goh, she said raising an eyebrow.

I don't know where this came from but I said, Do you want to get some coffee?

Sure, she said.

I told her I was in the process of a divorce. She told me that she'd already been divorced. It's rough, she said, but you'll get over it. She's on her second marriage. Gia said she's an appraiser and that's how she met her husband. Her husband is a real estate agent, named Martin Goh. She was appraising a house he was selling. Martin spends his Sundays showing houses in the Hollywood Hills, which leaves her Sundays to do what she pleases.

I'd meet Gia at Sunday yoga and we'd go out for coffee afterward. We did this for a couple of weeks.

Where do you live? She asked after drinking a mocha latte.

I have a little single apartment. Nothing to look at.

How would I know unless I see it?

I hadn't slept with another woman in over ten years. I would never have dreamed that I'd be sleeping with a married woman other than my wife. Then again, I never dreamed that I'd be getting a divorce. It's the worst thing I'd ever experienced, because I don't want my marriage to end. There doesn't seem to be anything wrong with my marriage, except that my wife lost interest in me, us, and the life we were building. She even alluded to never having loved me at all.

●

I rushed, Elise said. My wife cried, her head in her hands. Our kids were at her sister's. We sat in our kitchen, painted peach, a color that she loved. I rushed into getting married. I don't want to be married anymore. I don't know if I ever did.

She was thirty-one and I was thirty-two when we wed. We'd known each other for about a year when we decided to go for it. We agreed that we'd get married once she finished up her master's degree. She was the most beautiful bride. I still remember her coming down the aisle, coming to me, to be with me.

I love our kids and the family we created, Elise said, but I don't want to be married anymore. I can be a mother, but not a wife.

She swore up and down that I wasn't a bad husband or a bad father. She just wanted another life, one without me. I sat there quietly, staring down at the dark wood of the kitchen table, remembering the day she walked down the aisle. She lifted her veil and I thought I saw a smile. I thought it was beaming, our marriage sealed with a kiss. Maybe it wasn't beaming. Maybe it was forced, a tight smile on a woman who got married because a woman entering her thirties believed she should be married.

She was supposed to work after we got married, use that expensive degree of hers. We planned to save some money, then have a kid. Instead, we got pregnant months after our wedding. She gave birth to Brian, then Amanda, then Paul. She never used that degree.

I don't want to be one of those women who spent their lives caring for other people, Elise said, and not herself. I don't want to be a cliché like that. I'm forty-one now and I'm becoming a cliché.

I got up from the table, walked across the kitchen. There was a bowl of fruit on the counter. I picked it up and threw it across the room, the apples and bananas leaping into the air, then falling all over the floor.

But I'm happy! I said. I love my life. I love our life. AND I CAN'T BELIEVE YOU'RE RUINING IT ALL!!! YOU'RE

TURNING EVERYTHING UPSIDE DOWN!!!

She was frightened I could tell, but she didn't move. She knew no matter how angry I got, I'd never do anything to hurt her.

You're not the only one getting older, I said, trying to hold back the tears welling up in me.

She got up and ran toward me, embracing me. She wept into my chest, repeating, I'm sorry, I'm sorry, I'm sorry. I'm sorry that I want to be more than who I am.

I held her tight. I just held her.

●

Gia likes to have sex. I like having sex with Gia. We have sex after yoga on Sundays. Something that Gia does during sex is talk, have full blown conversations when we screw around. I was not used to this.

Why did you take up yoga? she asked while I made love to her.

Doctor's advice, I said in between breaths.

Hurt yourself?

Hurting myself. I'm used to more active sports.

Yoga is active, she said. Very active.

Not like sprinting, I said.

I orgasmed. So did she.

In my arms, she said, it's active staying in a pose, staying still.

I loved the smell of her perfume. My wife rarely wore perfume.

I said, Hey, do you want to meet for lunch sometime during the week? I can call you. We've been meeting all this time and you haven't given me your phone number.

She turned and looked at me. Her lovely face, serene and glowing. She said, I'm a married woman.

I'm a married man.

You're getting a divorce. I'm not…and I'm not going to get one.

●

Aw, crap, I said, tipping over, landing on my left side. I was determined to stand on my head, even if it killed me. I lay on the floor, wondering how Elise was doing. I knew she'd started a new job at a museum. Regardless, I still paid the mortgage on the house that I'm not living in and give money to raise children that I only see on Tuesday nights, Thursday nights, and Saturday afternoons.

I thought of my terrific job as Director of Sales, but the two times I was passed up for Vice President. I'm married to a woman who doesn't want to be with me and having sex with a woman who also doesn't want to be with me.

I looked around my small apartment. It's bare, just a bed. I hate sleeping alone in it. I'd always hated sleeping alone. Even when I was single I had roommates, the chatter of someone else in the home made me feel comfortable.

Elise said she didn't want to be a cliché: a woman who didn't think of herself and always cared for everyone. I didn't want to be a kind of cliché myself: a man who thought only of himself and didn't need anyone.

Even though my doctor instructed me not to, I put on my running shoes and headed out the door. I ran down Sunset past the fast-food joints and the used clothing stores. I ignored the

"Don't Walk" signals and kept on going. I ran into Hollywood, heaving and hurting, but I kept on going.

I stopped at Sunset and Western, bent over and vomited. I thought about my life and how unsatisfied I was with it. I thought about how I was supposed to be happily married and living in the suburbs. If Elise didn't want to be with me, maybe I need to be by myself. Just by myself.

When Elise came down the aisle at our wedding, I remembered her smile. I also remembered how I felt. I was relieved, so relieved. I was finally getting married. I didn't have to put up with the bullshit of the dating scene. Prior to Elise, I had had only two other girlfriends and didn't lose my virginity until I was twenty-one.

Elise was a great girl—smart, pretty, we wanted the same things. That was enough. She was enough for me. I thought I was enough for her. It just turned out that wasn't true. There was more and Elise was brave enough to realize it.

●

You're improving, said my yoga teacher. You were on your head for at least two seconds. I sat back up and smiled. The other members in class applauded, knowing I'd been struggling with standing on my head for quite some time now. The world looks different from that angle, doesn't it? My instructor chuckled. Off in the corner, Gia winked at me.

We closed the class in silent meditation. It was hard for me to meditate. All I could think about was having sex with Gia later in my apartment. On the walk to my car, I noticed Elise had left a message on my cell. She wanted me to call her back.

Hey, it's me, I said into the cell phone, trying to work the key into my car door. Are the kids all right?

Hi, she said. I just called to see how you were.

I'm fine. You?

She was quiet for a moment, then said, I got fired. I wasn't the right fit. I could hear the disappointment in her voice. This is what it means to try to be more than yourself, I thought. You get slammed sometimes.

There are other jobs out there, you know, I said. You'll land another one real soon.

She said, Do you want to come over a little later? I'll make something to eat for us. Maybe have a little family meal. The kids'll love it.

I saw Gia waving at me across the street. It was a wave that said she'd be seeing me in a few minutes. Her husband was out of town, so she could stay longer than the few hours we usually had.

I sorta made plans, I said.

Oh, okay, she said.

But I'll see you on Tuesday night when I pick up the kids from school.

I went to yoga class on Sunday and didn't see Gia. I was disappointed. I wanted to show her and everyone in class what I accomplished. Halfway during class, we were asked to do headstands.

I positioned my arms around my head and used the wall for support. I hoisted myself up and kept myself there. I'd never laughed upside down before, but I did. I saw my teacher nodding approvingly. I saw them all happy for me. Except for Gia.

I went to some of the night classes that she usually attended. She wasn't there either. I even asked the yoga studio about her. They told me that she had used up all of the classes that she'd bought. It looked like she didn't renew. After a few weeks, I decided to try and find her. One Sunday, I drove around the Hollywood Hills looking at real estate signs. There were a ton of them. Finally, I saw one that listed the agent as Martin Goh.

I drove to the house, an English Tudor at the top of a hill. A bald guy with black rimmed glasses, sporting a vintage suit, greeted me as I walked up the driveway. He was stocky and had a confident stride.

Beautiful day, he said. The kind of day that makes you wanna buy a house. He laughed, extending a hand. My name is Martin. What are you in the market for?

I, uh, am looking to buy in the area, I said.

Do you work in the industry?

Industry?

Entertainment. Movies.

No, in downtown. Sales.

Great. Let me show you around.

He took me on a tour of the mansion, a six-room home, with a den, library, and servants' quarters.

And out here, he said, is the dining room. As you can see it has a view of both the downtown skyline and, on a clear day, you can see all the way to the beach.

Amazing, I said. Is this a good neighborhood to raise a family?

Yeah, it's the best. There are some good private schools I can recommend. Not too many of the kids here go to public school.

I bet. You have kids?

No. My wife and I are content with just the two of us.

I have three kids. We're looking to move.

Well, this is the neighborhood to do it. What's your name again?

Peter Dantes.

Martin Goh stopped for a second. Are you going through a divorce?

Yes.

Were you the guy sleeping with my wife?

What?

It's all right. We're okay like that. Every once in a while, I'll head out of the roost. Gia's told me about you. Filipino guy with three kids, named Peter, getting a divorce. Are you really here to buy a house?

Actually no. I hadn't seen Gia in a while…

Yeah. She's like that. You met her in yoga, right? Six months ago, it was ceramics. Before that it was tennis. She likes to try new things.

I looked to the floor.

I hope you don't take her abrupt departure too seriously. That's what affairs are about.

I'd never had one. I wouldn't know.

Martin looked at me, almost with pity.

Can you do me a favor?

Sure.

Tell her I can stand on my head.

Huh?

It's a yoga thing. She'll understand.

A car horn was heard.

Excuse me. I think those are some serious buyers.

It was probably best that I never saw Gia again. I no longer get erections because of yoga. It just sort of stopped. I got into my car and drove away.

Guest List Girls

Surely, she would be invited this time. Surely, thought Elaine. Elaine had heard that her sorority sister Molly Cho would be marrying. Even though they hadn't spoken in a little while, and it had been some time before holiday cards had been exchanged, Elaine was certain—no, positive—that she would be invited to the wedding. So sure, in fact, that she picked out the wedding gift. It would be a silver platter from Tiff's. She knew that Molly would be registered at Tiffany's. And she knew that Molly would love that platter, a two-foot monstrosity with grape leaves emblazoned in the center.

She had received a newsletter, started by alumni from her sorority, that Molly Cho, a junior partner at Home Securities Bank, class of 1994, would marry investment banker Allan Chan in San Francisco. At least she won't have to change her initials, Elaine thought.

Since her graduation from the University of Southern California, Elaine had not kept in contact with some of her girlfriends like Addy Nealson and Rebecca Mar. Both of whom had gotten married and did NOT invite Elaine.

She shrugged it off. Weddings were expensive. Not everyone could be invited. She was made of stronger stuff; she wasn't going to fall apart just because she wasn't invited to a few of her insipid sorority sisters' weddings. It was no big deal. That's what she convinced herself.

Yet something loomed deep within her when she discovered she wasn't invited. It wasn't anything debilitating. She didn't take time off work to mourn the fact that she wasn't invited. She didn't shed a tear over not receiving an invitation. Oh, no, it wasn't anything like that. As a matter of fact, most times she didn't even think about it.

What she felt was simply an ache, a slight ache. It lasted 30 seconds—a minute at most. It came upon her at times when she was allowed to have a thought that was purely her own. When she was on the freeway, for example, and couldn't find a music station she liked, she turned off her radio, and thought. It bothered her: the idea that girls she went to school with, girls she had felt some kinship toward, girls she roomed with, did not want her at their nuptials. Then as quickly, she would think to herself: I couldn't have gone anyway; too busy, disavowing any notion that she was not, in the very least, wanted.

But we were friends! Elaine thought to herself. We did things together! Like when they were in college and went to The Window, a trendy downtown club—trendy because a European princess had vomited on the dance floor while dancing with her drug dealing boyfriend, trendy because there was a roped off entrance, trendy because there was a balcony that looked over the front door where you could see all of the losers who didn't have what it took to get into the club, people who lacked the look, the panache, that special something to separate you from the others in the crowd.

She made a point of only going to the Window with one of her girlfriends, justifying to herself that a girl alone would be too vulnerable. Her sorority sisters agreed. They would never go alone. Addy, a lovely half Asian, half white girl, agreed with that decision. Rebecca, a runner-up in the Miss Chinatown pageant, who had the presence of, well, a beauty contestant, nodded her head vigorously. Molly, a petite woman, doll-like, with exquisite skin said, "Without a doubt."

After they had all graduated, Elaine went straight into her graduate program at Pomona College. The other girls had gotten jobs, doing lord knows what, or had taken off to Europe to "bum around." It was in her second year at Pomona when she'd heard via Molly that Addy had gotten married.

"It was a lovely wedding," Molly said over lunch. "It was in Waikiki. By the beach. Seagulls flew above while they said their vows."

Seagulls? Elaine thought. They're scavengers, the rodents of the sky, no better than pigeons. Elaine wanted to say this. She was put off. It was also at that lunch that Molly let Elaine know that she would be moving back to San Francisco, a move that distanced their friendship.

There was no explanation as to why she wasn't invited to Addy's wedding. Elaine was slightly hurt but didn't really mind all that much. Addy and Elaine never really meshed. Addy being a laid-back girl from Hawaii, simply didn't click in with Elaine's urban, quickly-paced mentality.

"I'd be happy with a B, maybe even a C, as long as I pass," Addy once said of a class. Elaine envied Addy for saying that. Elaine would have loved the luxury of being able to settle for a "C." She couldn't possibly do that. More importantly, the Hunter Scholastic Society, which provided tuition for inner city youth, wouldn't settle for that. Elaine's education was paid for by HSS. They would pay her collegiate ride (with the exception of room and board), as long as she maintained a minimum of a 3. 2 grade point average. She had left college with an overall GPA of 3.8.

Elaine had an idea as to why she wasn't invited to Addy's wedding: Addy probably believed Elaine couldn't afford the trip to Hawaii. So many times in college, her girlfriends suggested a sojourn during spring break. Miami? Jamaica? Acapulco? Elaine declined, claiming work. Which was true. She had to earn room and board somehow. All the girls understood, except Addy.

"Don't you ever want to go anywhere?" Addy said, almost whining.

"Of course," Elaine said. "It's just now is not the time."

Addy used her father's Mastercard to no end, buying groceries, paying for gas, running up a tab at The Window.

Elaine didn't consider Addy's wedding a big loss. Through her college years with Addy, they had some good times, but would never be seen as close. Yes, they were roommates, but not the dearest of friends. Their interaction was cordial, usually friendly. They had gossiped, eaten each other's leftovers. Her fondest memory of Addy was when they dressed each other in togas—sheets pulled from their beds—to attend a party for the new pledges of their sorority. Elaine fixed her hair, swept it up into a French twist. In front of the mirror, Elaine looked at Addy, then at herself, for a moment, she truly felt like Addy's sister.

She really didn't mind all that much that she was left off the invitation list to Addy's wedding. That moment in front of the mirror was fleeting, perhaps a moment Addy wouldn't even recall.

But Molly. Molly! She had had many moments with Molly

that would never be described as fleeting. She helped Molly decide what she'd wear to the first exchange between her sorority and their brother fraternity, the Chis. She was the person Molly confided in when Molly had thoughts of leaving the sorority, because too many of the girls were stuck-up. Elaine convinced her that being in their sorority, one of the finest Asian American sororities in the country, had its advantages, namely the prestigious alums who could help them out in the future. That was the sole purpose for why Elaine joined. Past alums included influential businesswomen, a few senators, a best-selling author, and a famous news anchor.

Elaine was there (in the next room) when Molly lost her virginity to Peter Nguyen president of the Chi's pledge class. She was there for Molly when she discovered she was NOT pregnant with Peter's child. Elaine read out the directions of the home pregnancy kit herself.

"Thank God!" Molly screamed. And, of course, Molly received her period the following week.

Surely, she would be invited to Molly's wedding.

Through her sorority newsletter, she'd discovered that Rebecca Mar had gotten married. Rebecca Mar, who Elaine would later refer to as: That Stupid Chinese Princess from Monterey Park. Of course she never said that to her face, never. She would never tell the most bubbly girl in their class and also a first runner up in the Miss Chinatown pageant that she thought Rebecca Mar was just plain stupid. To have done that, particularly in college would have spelled social death! Everyone liked Rebecca, liked her enthusiasm, liked her rich black hair with streaks of honey brown. Honey brown bought from a bottle, although Rebecca said they were natural.

Elaine didn't DISLIKE Rebecca. As a matter of fact, in college Elaine was an outwardly good friend, always supportive.

"Do you think I look fat?" Rebecca asked dressing for an exchange with another fraternity. Elaine will never forget that dress, blood red with shimmering sequins, a hemline that went up to here, a neckline that plunged down to there. She'd never seen a dress like that or would she ever. That dress was handmade, as were all of Rebecca's dresses. Sometimes when she was alone in the apartment, Elaine would look into Rebecca's closet and marvel at the clothes. (Her other roomies had fine dresses, too. Elaine gasped at what they paid for a bra.)

"Really, do I look fat?" Rebecca said again.

"Don't be ridiculous," Elaine said. "You couldn't gain an ounce of weight if you tried." Elaine genuinely believed this. Elaine had witnessed Rebecca devour a whole bag of Doritos and a foot long burrito in one sitting, then eat a burger an hour later. Elaine saw Rebecca eat a whole tray of hors d'oeuvres at The Window, leaving to dance a bit, then coming back to eat half a tray of sushi.

Elaine, however, was conscious of her weight. She wasn't fat really. Maybe slightly plump. She had a thin—very thin—layer of fat that rode around her waist when she wore her favorite jeans. She had full thighs, but not fat. She wore miniskirts a few times in school, confident of her legs.

There was one strong bond she had with Rebecca. They were exercise partners. They made aerobics class five times a week when they were in school, always standing next to each other in the gym. When aerobics wasn't available, they went running. Elaine liked studying with Rebecca. Rebecca always worked hard, had dreams of owning her own accounting firm by the time she was thirty.

Elaine liked that kind of ambition. Elaine and Rebecca checked each other's papers before it was turned in.

Rebecca had well thought out essays. (As opposed to Addy's that seemed to be shoddily put together.) Rebecca's grammar was flawless, simply flawless! Elaine had nothing but respect for Rebecca, a smart, pretty girl with a glowing personality. It wasn't until the party held at Rebecca's family restaurant, the Jade Lantern, that Elaine's respect began to die, forever brandishing her with the nickname: That Stupid Chinese Princess from Monterey Park.

The Jade Lantern was a restaurant shaped like a Pagoda. Goldfish swam in a large aquarium by the double door entrance. The carpet was a festival red and paper lanterns hung from the ceiling. Although it was a Friday night, a big money maker for any restaurant, it was shut down for the exchange between the Sigmas and the Chis.

Elaine witnessed Rebecca yelling at an elderly Chinese man, "There was too much oil in the food." "I wanted *red* streamers to go with the lanterns, not orange." "Why wasn't there valet?" "I wanted the napkins to look like flowers, not triangles." "Couldn't the food be brought in any faster?" "Couldn't you hire people who spoke better English?" "Fix your hair, you always look tired." The Chinese man simply nodded, looking up at Rebecca.

When the exchange ended, Elaine and Molly stayed to confirm that the party went well and congratulated Rebecca on her work. Molly did most of the talking, Elaine held a tight smile and mostly nodded.

"You think it was okay?" Rebecca asked, standing in the lobby, putting on her coat, her face pleading for recognition.

"It was greeeeeat!" Molly answered.

Rebecca sighed, "If you say so." The elderly Chinese man entered the lobby. "Dad!" she called to him, "I'm leaving." The Chinese man nodded.

Her Father! Elaine mentally gasped. Belittling an employee in front of everyone was bad enough, belittling your father was another story. On the ride home, Elaine silently fumed, grateful she was sitting in the back seat, hoping Molly (who was driving) and Rebecca (who fell asleep in the front passenger seat) couldn't see her face. Elaine didn't want them to see her contorted facade, eyes moist with tears, hiding a disgusted and disappointed interior. Her father, Elaine thought, Rebecca's dad worked so she can have parties and afford handmade dresses and go to that expensive college…and she treated him that way. Her father!

Elaine would, could never treat her father in such a manner. As a small child, she'd wait for her dad to return from work. She'd have a 7-up ready for him as soon as she saw him approaching. She'd stand behind him, massaging his shoulder—mainly the right shoulder, the one he carried the heavy bottles with, replenishing Segal's Mountain Fresh Water in the suburbs.

In a quiet whisper, Elaine focused on Rebecca's sleeping head, and uttered, "You stupid, stupid girl."

Elaine looked down at her lap, then up again, just in time to catch Molly looking away from her in the rearview mirror.

●

Elaine stood at her mailbox, almost sweating. Molly's wedding was five weeks away. Surely she would get an invitation. She fumbled for her keys, looking for the one that would open her mailbox.

When she was looking to buy a home, she pictured a little house somewhere in the hills. A little cottage perhaps with a mailbox on the lawn, the kind of mailbox with a little red flag the mailman pulled up when he delivered. She wanted a lawn with rose bushes, maybe lilies. She imagined a bay window she would look out of with a view of a serene little street. She wanted a charming little garage, an old-fashioned garage that you had to get out of your car to open.

Her neighbors would be almost well-to-do, not garishly rich, but comfortable. They would be neighbors who showed promise in their careers, executive types perhaps. They would be well educated, at least college graduates. They would read books, mainly literary fiction, none of that new-age shit. They would be conservatively liberal, moderate Democrats maybe, and a nice mix of Christians and Jews.

Unfortunately, she wasn't able to live in such a home or neighborhood. She lived in Hollywood, east Hollywood exactly, in a one-bedroom house that she rented. Her neighbors spoke English with an accent and were college educated in countries like Russia, Turkey, Korea, or Thailand. She hoped to live in a neighborhood with more white people but the Armenians would have to do.

Elaine made good money, very good money in fact, and even though her undergraduate work was paid for, she took out loans for graduate school putting her thousands of dollars in debt, money she vowed to pay back in the next seven years.

Elaine stood by her mailbox, a black metal thing, attached to a gray metal fence surrounding her front yard. She lifted the black top of the mailbox then pulled out her letters. She went into her home, leafing through the mail, hoping to find that white envelope made of fine parchment inviting her to Molly's wedding.

There was a gas bill, a flyer announcing a missing child, an invitation to apply for a new credit card, a yellow envelope from Publisher's Clearinghouse suggesting that she could be the next winner, and a letter from Kaiser Hospital. She knew that letter was requesting payment for her father's physical therapy. Her father's insurance allowed fifteen free visits, anything after that required a co-pay of thirty dollars. The fifteen free visits were used up quickly. Elaine insisted that her father go every week at her expense until his shoulder healed. She would help out with the mortgage until he got back on his feet.

But there was no invitation from Molly.

She threw the mail onto her plaid couch, kicked off her shoes then went into the kitchen for something to drink. She looked out her kitchen window with a view of an alley and sighed.

Elaine went back into her living room with Ikea bought furniture and a throw rug from Crate and Barrel to cover the shag carpet. She got on her computer, logged on, and did an internet search, finding a site for the San Francisco white pages. If she found the number, she would call. If it's in the white pages, it'll be a landline phone, not a cell. Her number wouldn't pop up on their end. She found the number, logged off, picked up her phone, punched in the 415 area code, specific to San Francisco, and dialed the remaining seven digits.

The phone rang and a male voice answered.

"Hi, is Molly home?"

"No, she's at a dress fitting," he said.

"Is this Allan? Her soon to be husband?" She wanted to sound cheerful, nonchalant.

"Um, yeah, who's this?"

"I'm just a friend. I went to school with Molly— "

"Cool. Are you coming to the wedding?"

"Well, actually, I just had one class with her. She wouldn't remember me. I heard from a friend of a friend that she was getting married. So I thought I'd call." She laughed, a high-pitched laugh that nauseated her.

"Okay, do you want me to have her call you? She'll be back in an hour."

"Uh, I'll call back then."

"All right. Who is this?"

Elaine hung up before she could respond. There was a time when Elaine called Molly and they would talk on the phone for hours. When Elaine went up north for Christmas or Easter break in college, Elaine would call or Molly would call and they would talk, just about things, frivolous things like what classes they would like to take together or how some of the incoming pledges showed real promise.

She didn't even have to say her name. Molly could identify her by the sheer sound of her "Hello." There was a set familiarity. In her job, she kept cards with her wherever she went, her identity summed up in a little 2x3 piece of paper stating her profession: Accounts Manager.

There was a time when her world was college and sorority sisters and she told them everything. Well, almost everything.

She never told them that one night she went to The Window by herself (she had a night class and the girls had gone ahead; she said she would catch them at the club later). She approached the roped off entrance, the doorman said, "Are you on the guest list?"

"No, but my friends are inside."

"So, you're not on the guest list."

"My friends are waiting for me."

The doorman looked her up and down. He was sizing her up, she knew. She became nervous, touching her hair, feeling the temperature of her body rise. She had never had a problem getting in before, but she was always with one of her sorority sisters. The doormen looked at them and simply assumed they were on the guest list. Addy, Rebecca, and Molly were girls who had the presence of being on a guest list.

She could see the doorman's face. He was deciding, deciding whether she was one of them: the type of girl who deserved to get into the hottest club in town, the type of girl that Addy or Rebecca or Molly obviously were.

Elaine thought of Addy and tried something that she saw her do. Elaine smiled and said, "Oh, sweetie, please let me in. I gotta sit down, these heals are killing me. Please, please, please?" Elaine even pursed her lips the way she'd seen Addy do when trying to get out of a difficult situation, say convincing a cop to let her go after speeding.

"If you're not on the list, miss," the doorman said.

Elaine thought of Rebecca, pushed out her chest, and put her hand on the doorman's arm, caressing his bare skin with her middle finger. She saw Rebecca do that to a bartender so she could get free drinks for the evening. "Oh, Mr. Doorman," she said, "I'll be your new best friend if you let me in."

The doorman pulled away and said, "Sorry. You'll have to wait."

Elaine thought of Molly, pristine Molly. All Molly had to do was look sad and everyone came to comfort her. When she was at a bookstore looking for a book that the store didn't have, she looked down, almost in tears. The cashier, in an attempt to cheer up the poor sop of a girl, said, I can put a rush order in and your book will be here tomorrow.

Elaine sighed, looked down and said in a broken voice, "But my friends are inside."

"Sweetie, there are lots of people out here you can make friends with. You're not on the list."

She waited.

Of course, the fucking doorman let other girls in without checking his list, his goddamned, fucking guest list! Bustier girls, big-haired girls, girls oozing out of their tiny black dresses, girls who carelessly laughed, girls who stepped out of limousines, glamorous girls who didn't try to be glamorous. Girls of privilege who didn't know they were privileged which made fucking doormen unhook the fucking red rope at the mere sight of one of them approaching.

Elaine stood, arms crossed, waiting. She looked up and saw her girlfriends, Molly, Addy, Rebecca on the balcony. She hoped they could not see her. She slid into the shadows, watching them laugh with somewhat attractive men.

The doorman knew, Elaine thought. He knew that she was not one of those girls, one of those guest list girls. There was a scent she gave off somehow, a way she walked, or titled her head—something—that let the doorman—or everyone else for that matter—know that she could not, would not get in.

After waiting an hour, she went home. When her sorority sisters returned asking her why she didn't meet them at The Window, she feigned a yawn and said, "Wasn't up to it tonight."

●

The phone rang. Elaine picked it up, and wearily said, "Hello?"

"Hi," a voice said, "This is Molly, you called?"

Elaine gripped the phone, wanting to die, die of sheer embarrassment. Her eyes bulged and she repeatedly hit her forehead with the palm of her hand. Silently mouthing the words: shit, shit, SHIT! Her fiancé must have told her some woman called, an old classmate, someone she barely knew.

"Hello?" Molly said.

Elaine clicked the "off" button on her phone and threw it across the room. She hid in a corner, covering her face with her hands, peaking through the crack of her fingers. The phone rang again. She could hear it ringing across the room. Elaine thought of it as a cancer ready to eat her insides away. Just let it ring, Elaine thought. Molly would eventually hang up. Go away, Elaine thought, go away! A frightful thought entered her head. Her voice mail greeting! Elaine had a mental seizure, knowing the machine would pick up with the message, "Hi, you've reached Elaine. Not in right now but listen for the beep."

She had to face this. Yes. She would face this. She ran to the phone, picked it up and said, "Hello. Hello, hello."

"Hello," Molly said. "We were disconnected."

"Uh, yes, how did you get my number? I didn't leave one?"

"Oh, I have this little box that is attached to my home phone. It records the numbers of people who called. It helps with telemarketers," she laughed.

"Molly," Elaine said and had a brilliant idea: she would identify herself as Jenny or Cathy or Hortense from Freshman Comp— remember me? I heard you were getting married and wanted to say, That's great. Okay, bye.

"Yes, this is Molly. Who is this?"

"This is…," Elaine was going to say Jenny, but thought otherwise. This wasn't Addy or Rebecca; it was Molly, a guest-list-girl she was once close to. "It's Elaine."

There was a brief pause.

"Elaine," Molly said, "How ARE you?"

"I'm fine. I'd read in the newsletter you were getting married. I wanted to congratulate you."

"Thank you, thank you. I wanted to send you an invitation but didn't know how to contact you."

You could have tried, Elaine thought. It took all of twenty minutes to find you on the internet. "That's okay. Hey, Molly?"

"Yes?"

"I wanna ask you something. It's kinda silly, but— "

"You can ask me anything you want, Elaine."

"Do you know why I wasn't invited to Addy and Rebecca's weddings?"

"Well, I don't know, honey. You'd have to ask them."

"I'm just curious."

"I was surprised not to see you there myself."

"Tell me the truth, Molly. Tell me as the girl who sat along with you when you discovered you were not pregnant with Peter's kid.

Did you purposely not invite me to your wedding?"

Silence.

"Elaine, why are we talking like this? How are you? It's been--"

"Why didn't you invite me? Just curious?"

Molly sighed. "I was planning on inviting you. I really was, but I talked it over with my girlfriends."

I used to be a girlfriend, too, Elaine thought. "What girlfriends?"

"You know, Addy and Rebecca. Please don't tell them I told you this."

"I don't see them anyway. What does it matter?"

"Well, it's just that…well, Addy and Rebecca are uncomfortable around you, Elaine."

"They hate me."

"No, honey, nothing like that. It's just that, well, you know how you can be. I was never bothered by it, but they are."

"By what?"

"Well, Elaine, it's just that…well, you know…you think you're better than everybody."

Elaine gulped. I think I'm better than everybody? Me? They think I'm a snob? Elaine offered, "No, that's not true."

"You came from this bad neighborhood—"

"Lay off my neighborhood. Anyway, it wasn't bad." Well, not THAT bad, Elaine knew. Perhaps the homes in her neighborhood weren't well kept, maybe there was graffiti, and a patrolling gang or two, but neighbors liked each other, looked out for one another. The families, albeit working class, seemed happy—at least outwardly so. For these reasons, Elaine thought she grew up in a good neighborhood, a fine environment.

"Well, you came from this place where you thought you were

better. You worked harder, you were smarter, sacrificed more. Acted superior kind of."

"I never said anything like that."

"Well, people can feel that, you know. I didn't mind that. They're really admirable qualities. But you kind of exude an air of superiority. Like you went further than the other girls did."

"I did go further. Jumping from working to middles class is a higher leap than beginning in middle class and simply staying there."

"You see what I mean? It came to the point that Addy couldn't tell you what fun she had in Europe or the dress that Rebecca had made was something she loved because you thought those things were nothing. You had more important things to do like getting your graduate degree or finding a good job."

"But education and work are more important than trips to Europe or a dress."

"Sure, it is, honey, but not to other people. I guess that's what I'm trying to say, you don't value other people's lives."

"I would value their lives if they were doing anything with it."

Elaine heard Molly sigh. She could see Molly rubbing one of her temples.

"What I mean is," Elaine said, trying to start over, "that I never believed Addy or Rebecca valued me or what I was doing."

There was a pause that Elaine could feel, an anxious pause that Molly was waiting to be filled. "Did you stop to think about that, Molly? I had to work and all Addy asked me was why? I needed to maintain a certain grade point average so I could stay in school and Addy was satisfied with C's so she could leach off her family and go dancing at The Window. My parents worked hard and so did Rebecca's, but Rebecca never saw that. She couldn't see past her dresses or her parties."

"What did you think of me?" Molly asked.

Elaine looked up at her ceiling, her white stucco ceiling and said, "I thought you were my good friend." She looked down at her linoleum. "I know we're not good friends anymore. It's been a while. I thought you understood me. And…and I thought you'd understand that I would want to go to your wedding, even though it's been some time since we've talked. Because little things like being invited just means something."

It means, she wanted to say, but didn't articulate that there is a small separation from someone like me and someone like you. There were girls who got into clubs and those who had to wait outside, maybe not get in at all. Those girls who eyed the doorman, leaning forward when that rope, guarding the entrance to a club, made you okay, made you worthy. There were girls who got to go to weddings and others who wondered why they weren't invited.

"I didn't mean to hurt your feelings, Elaine. Honey."

There were girls who were born more fortunate and girls born with less. And girls born with less looked at the fortunate girls and wondered why couldn't that have been me?

Just before you think you're going to get what the other girls had, something happens like your dad gets hurt on the job, throwing out a shoulder and getting a bad back for lifting heavy things all day. Your mother's a teacher's aide who makes a shitty salary and is getting old. So part of the salary you work for goes to paying for doctor visits insurance won't cover or paying off school loans to get that extra degree to give you that extra edge over the competition. Then you end up in a neighborhood similar to the one you grew up in, because that's all you can afford. You wonder if you'll ever become that girl you hoped to be, that kind of girl you envied in college. The one who gets in. The one who gets invited.

"Elaine, I'd like for you to come to my wedding."

There, she said it. You got invited. You were invited to the goddamned wedding. Are you happy now?

"I'll put your name down on the guest list. Right now. I'll write it down."

She wasn't happy, wasn't happy at all.

"Will it just be you, Elaine? Or will you be bringing someone?"

Elaine was proud that she'd gone on, created a life for herself, a life that she worked hard for, years away from college and stupid party days. Still. This phone conversation confirmed it. She was still the girl outside, outside and waiting.

"There, you're on the guest list. Will it just be you, Elaine? Elaine?"

With the phone tucked between her ear and her shoulder, Elaine didn't know how to respond.

Tito Abalez on the Brink of Manhood

Tito Abalez had the option of having his parents watch in court or wait in the hall. He chose to have them absent while he testified. He nodded to the bailiff (who was also Filipino). The bailiff escorted Mr. and Mrs. Abalez out.

Tito didn't want them to hear the whole story. His parents knew; the police told them. He wasn't sure what the police said exactly, but he was confident it was enough of the truth. He knew his parents, especially his father, couldn't take hearing the facts coming from Tito's mouth.

Last year, when the Los Angeles police brought him home, Tito went to his room and heard the murmurs through the wall. He heard his mother scream then burst into tears, repeating, "No, no, NO."

He didn't hear his father say anything, do anything, but Tito knew his dad was sitting, arms crossed, face like a rock, taking it all in. He heard the police drive away.

His father opened Tito's door (Dad, or "dod" as Tita called him, never knocked when entering a room in his house), and said, "We have to go to the fundraiser at St. Theresa's. Get dressed. Wear your *barong*."

Tito went into his closet and looked at his clothes. He always wore the things his mother bought for him, even though they sometimes didn't fit, even though they sometimes weren't cool. He wore the jeans that were not Levis. He wore the shirts that were not Lightning Bolt. He wore the shoes that were not Vans. And, when there were special events, special Filipino events, he grudgingly wore his barong, a sheer long-sleeved shirt made of piña cloth.

Before he dressed, he wanted to bathe, had the need to cleanse himself, remove the day from his body, wipe the small specks of blood on his legs. He stood in the shower, steam rising above his head, when he saw his father's figure enter the bathroom. A white plastic curtain separated them, and Tito witnessed his father's ominous dark silhouette grow larger as he walked closer to the shower.

"What happened?" Dod asked.

Even though his father could not see him, Tito turned away, streams of water pelting his head, rivulets running down his body.

"Well...," Tito began. He watched the water accumulate at his feet, eventually circling, then disappearing down the drain. He grabbed his thing—his crotch, he came to know it now as his crotch—and lowered his head. A gloom had settled into his soul because he knew his father was unhappy and would be unhappy for a long time. He knew, at twelve, that something had gone wrong and it would affect his days, affect his relationship with Dod forever. Dod who worked as a security guard, protecting whole buildings by himself, but could not protect his own son.

"What happened?" Dod asked again.

"I was at the beach...with some friends. I got lost...." The words were boulders in his throat. But before he could finish, he saw his father's silhouette shrink, then disappear with a click of the doorknob.

He kept his hand on his crotch, observing the few strands of pubic hair there. He rubbed his crotch, and watched it grow. There was power there, he discovered. Boys becoming men know there is comfort there as well.

●

Tito sat on the wooden pews of the courtroom, wearing a navy coat and a striped tie. It was the same coat and tie he wore to his first Holy Communion three years earlier. He had outgrown them, but his parents couldn't afford to buy new ones. He felt the tightness of the coat on his body, particularly around his shoulders, and he adjusted the tie because it kept rising above his navel.

He waited to testify, to tell the story again. He had told it so much, to so many people--police, then more police, then doctors, then psychiatrists, then lawyers--that he could ramble it out while sleeping. Some of the lawyers tried to confuse him, changing sequences around, but Tito was in seventh grade now. He knew better. He wasn't some little fourth grader you could push around. He recognized the fact that there were some pretty mean people out there. Meaner than some of the gang members who wrote their names on the walls of his neighborhood, meaner than the guy who shot Mr. Cho at the liquor store a few blocks away.

He wouldn't budge when the lawyers tried to confuse him. He stated the story exactly the way it happened--except maybe for a little part of it he kept to himself. The little part that no one needed to know anyway.

Dod told him not to tell the story when Mr. Jimenez from next door or Mrs. Tolentino from across the street asked why police brought Tito home wrapped in nothing but a towel, his white underwear still damp from the beach. Dod told him to shut up and go about like nothing happened when kids at school heard about it, too. He learned to look straight ahead and hear nothing, feel nothing, when Joey Ramos and Milton Gilberto, guys who used to be his friends, pointed at him when he walked down the halls.

The only person at school who was kind was Miss Tombayo, his school counselor. She asked him if there was any way she could help: his grades were sliding. He shook his head, No.

She leaned toward him from her desk, and he saw the dark shadow between her breasts. He started to cry because Miss Tombayo was so pretty and he'd wanted to be close to her since he'd begun junior high. She had long black hair that rode on her shoulders and brown skin a tinge lighter than his own.

She sat next to him, bringing a box of Kleenex. She brought his head to her chest, and he felt the round curves of her bosom, and was surprised at how a woman's body could make things right again. He sniffed her, and didn't realize that she was wearing perfume, assuming women always smelled that fragrant. He decided that he loved Mrs. Tombayo and always will. He felt his crotch tingle, believing that love and that tingle might be one and the same.

The school bell rang, but he didn't want to leave. Miss Tombayo told him everything will be all right. She wiped the tears from his face, her long nails scraping his skin. He left to go to his last class, his favorite class, English.

He thought of her hands on his face, remembering Mom doing the same when he only had one digit in his age. Mom who peered into his room before he nodded off to sleep. Mom who broke into tears when the police told her what happened.

He thought women could be frail, not strong like his dad, yet in that frailty his heart sank. He wanted nothing more than to save them, from the sadness and ugliness that he knew existed out there. He had felt lost and weak since the police brought him home; but he surmised, nothing was more vulnerable than a weeping woman.

●

Tito was asked to point to the man who "victimized" him. He pointed to a brown haired gentleman, surrounded by three men in suits. The judge thanked him. Tito sat down.

He listened to lawyers and experts and character witnesses, witnesses like the wife. She claimed her husband was a good man, regardless of everything, and their family would suffer. A very respected businessman, she called him. A good father, she also said. And when she left the stand, passing Tito to enter the hallway, she looked at him as if it were his fault for doing this to her, to her family.

He listened to experts speaking of these kinds of men being primarily heterosexual, preying on a child regardless of the child's gender, seeking only control. Tito stared at the floor, feeling alone. Maybe this was a bad idea, he wondered. Maybe I shouldn't have said anything, just gone back to my life.

"They prey on children," the lawyer said.

Tito misunderstood "prey" for "pray." Tito had seen his father pray to a child.

Once Tito walked into the living room and found his father on his knees weeping in front of the Baby Jesus, a small statue adorned in a red cape and crown. His father was praying for strength— his father always prayed for strength, strength to endure his boss who was 15 years younger, strength in knowing that leaving the Philippines was the right decision, even if it meant abandoning what could have been a prominent career in law.

"It was tough that decision I made," Dod once said, hinting that there will be a time, maybe even several times, when a boy must make a manly choice.

Tito watched earnestly as his father mumbled prayers to the Christ Child, a child that would grow to be a God. Tito knew his father never prayed in church, never to the adult Jesus, emaciated on the cross, a world-weary Jesus with pain in His eyes. Dod prayed to the Babe, knowing even a deity knew more innocent days. What decision does a God make that forces Him to leave his boyhood behind forever? Tito wondered.

Tito did not know the answer, but he had an inkling when the district attorney called him and his parents into a cold office, posing the question: "Will you let your son testify?" The DA asked Dod and Mom for permission. Mrs. Abalez said "No" emphatically, said it would be too difficult for a twelve-year-old boy to do. "He had gone through enough already," she said.

Tito adored his mother, loved her, witnessed her endurance at pulling double shifts at the supermarket where she worked as a cashier. When he was small, he massaged her back by walking on it. Now, too big, he used his hands to massage her, pulled her knuckles, rubbed her palms, trying to get blood flowing through fingers that pushed register keys all day. Most times, he would rather spend time with her than with Dod, a man lacking affection, lacking the knowledge to stroke a child's head when he came home. He was not like his mother who stood up for her child, ached for him in some cases.

Dod did not respond to the DA's request for testimony. Tito knew, instinctively knew his father was waiting. He was waiting for Tito to speak, to choose. For as much as he loved his mother, she knew nothing of becoming a man. Frankly, neither did Tito. But in the DA's office, with walls cluttered with citations and degrees, Tito felt he was at a precipice, felt it was time to make a manly decision.

Hoping to sway Tito's decision, the DA went on to explain that the man who did this, who did this to children was a Santa Monica businessman who had a history of predatory behavior. He pursued minority children, mainly Latino or Asian, because he assumed these children wouldn't necessarily speak English that well and be unable to convey what happened. Or if the children did speak, did tell their parents, they would be too afraid to report it because immigrants have a nature to stay quiet.

Tito flinched when the DA used the word "rape" during the trial. He did not know what rape meant exactly. He knew it was often referred to women. He was not a woman. No one knew, except maybe Dod, just how much of a man Tito had become.

After his testimony in front of the judge, he could have left the courtroom. But he didn't want to enter the hallway where his parents were waiting. He didn't want to see them just yet. He wanted to see what he did to the Santa Monica businessman, wanted to see what kind of sentence he would get. Tito's words had made all the difference in the world, truth from his mouth. would send him away.

When it was over, he went into the hallway and took off his coat and tie, clothes that could no longer contain him. He walked to his parents sitting at the end of the hall. They looked at him, wondering what to do.

"Let's go," Tito said.

They drove home quietly in their blue Toyota pick-up. Tito sat between his parents, and watched the rosary dangle from the rearview mirror.

They stopped at McDonald's for a Big Mac, and he knew everything would be all right. Dod only bought food at McDonald's after church, and he knew by ordering a Big Mac with large fries, his parents, especially his father, let him know that they don't blame him.

At home, they sat on the couch, saying nothing. It became clear to Tito that this would never be mentioned again. Three months later, at Summer's end, the Abalez family moved to the San Fernando Valley. Tito learned when things get too painful, too rough, starting over is sometimes best.

●

A year before the trial, Tito went to the beach with his friends. They took the bus to Venice beach. His friends took off their clothes and put on swimming trunks. Tito wore only his underwear. In elementary school, he thought nothing of stripping down to his briefs to play in the water. His friends laughed at him for not bringing trunks. Tito became embarrassed, choosing to play at the far end of the shore, not realizing he'd lost track of his friends and his clothes.

He bounced in the water, enjoying the revitalizing effect of the sea. He floated, like a fetus in a womb, enjoying the sun and the slight turbulence of the waves. He was free, away from his parents and his so-called friends who laughed at him for wearing his underwear.

He left the waves and searched for his belongings. He spotted men in black uniforms some distance away. Even at the beach, he couldn't escape cops. Cops in black and white cars circled his neighborhood. Here, however, they rode bikes and only one or two black and white cars were spotted.

He walked up and down the shore, looking for his friends and, for the very first time, he felt naked. Men and women watched him as he passed. Tito believed they were making fun of him, pitying him. They somehow knew he was a Filipino kid from the bad part of LA who didn't know the difference between swimming trunks and underwear. He looked down to avoid their eyes, walking briskly, periodically gazing up, searching for markers of his friends, perhaps a flash of that green bed sheet they placed their clothes on. He felt the eyes of strangers sear right through him. In his mind, they were laughing at him.

He didn't know that only a few people saw him. A woman in a large, brimmed hat saw him. A lifeguard saw him. A black girl, a few years older than he, saw him. Three, only three people really spotted him. People could sense potential, could see if young people will mature well. There is an inherent nature in people, easily spotting the runts from the winners. They knew this boy, in his white underwear, was on the brink of manhood. Tito's body was developing, and, unknown to him, anyone looking at him knew he would someday make a fine masculine image. His slender body revealed developing muscles on his torso. His legs were already sturdy. His hours in the sun added a sheen to his skin, as if the golden rays massaged glitter into his flesh.

They thought this boy, with an already splendid figure, would grow to a splendid figure of a man. They knew in a few years, he would be handsome, and in ten years, he would be stunning.

Tito noticed women on the beach tanning, and his thing tugged at him. He felt himself growing. He thought of Miss Tombayo, hoping he would see her first thing Monday morning. He had always liked her. He felt a warmth fill his head, his body, causing him to sweat through the palms when he saw her. He imagined someday marrying her and making her a good husband and buying her things and bringing her flowers and doing all that he can to make her happy. Simply thinking of her made him fully grown.

He walked into the bathroom, went to a urinal to relieve himself. He didn't notice the man—the man in a brown sweatshirt— standing next to him, looking at him, looking at his thing. He felt uncomfortable and walked away, but the man—who was a good foot taller than he—grabbed him by the shoulder, turned him around, pulled him into a bathroom stall, forced him onto a toilet, and pulled down his underwear. The man put his head between Tito's legs.

Tito resisted, pushed him away, and said, "Stop it." The

man held Tito firmly. Tito kicked, his legs getting caught in his underwear.

"Let me taste your crotch," the man said. But Tito hit him, smashed his face, hearing a small crack when he punched the nose. The man was undeterred. It seemed Tito was being eaten alive, he felt a warm wet feeling swirling around down there. He screamed. He was ashamed of screaming; he let the world know he was vulnerable.

He thought of his father.

He noticed feet gathering around the stall, a policeman stood at the doorway, and grabbed the man by the shoulders.

"Fucking pervert!" the Cop said, and the man released himself from Tito. Tito sat on the toilet; his underwear still caught around his ankles. He cried. He shouldn't have cried. Boys becoming men don't cry.

Police surrounded the bathroom. One of them gave Tito a towel then sat him in the back seat of the car. He was taken to a police station and asked questions. He answered them, saying things like: he pushed me, he forced me. And the cops looked sympathetic. He told them everything.

On his ride home, shivering in his towel, he did not tell them what he was feeling. They didn't want to know what he was feeling, just what happened. It was good they didn't, he thought. He would have said he was scared or he was mad or he was confused. What he wouldn't tell them was, for a brief moment, with a glint of sun passing his eyes, he discovered something; for a small second, he became aware of his thing—his crotch—and the kind of feelings that resided there. He could not convey with words what it was like to have this man, before him, this stranger on his knees. When the police grabbed the man, he looked up with confusion. Their eyes met and Tito was startled at the blueness of the man's eyes, startled by the red blood falling from his nose, blood he caused by punching the nose. The blood leaked onto his legs. Tito was horrified yet satisfied that he had done *some* damage.

Tito's eyes welled with tears. He shut them, feeling empty, feeling cold, and he pushed his mind far away, away to a point of blankness, entering that dark unfeeling space boys becoming men are familiar with because there is comfort there.

Music Heard in Hi-Fi

The soundtrack of *Maybe Someday* was first heard in a small house on Vendome Avenue. It was eventually heard in homes on Council, Reno, Dillon, and Union. The music of this hit Broadway musical was heard in cars driving north on Rampart, turning right on Temple Street, then stopping at a parking lot in Bahay Kubo, a popular hang out in Historic Filipinotown—Hi-FI for short—in Los Angeles, Ca. At Bahay Kubo, the music of *Maybe Someday* was heard on the loudspeakers, a boot-legged video of the musical played on a large TV in the restaurant.

Filipino men and women sang along, including the old *manongs* and *manangs* who sang in cracked, weathered voices. Middle age women—who had lost their virginities decades before—sang the tunes of the musical about an innocent girl stuck in a horrible, senseless war.

They knew the songs because the story was told and told and told again. Jethro and Goldstein, the producers for this musical about the Vietnam War were on a worldwide search for a cast, especially the leading lady. Auditions were held on three continents. The lead and a good number of the supporting cast and chorus were found in the Philippines.

Bless Velasco knew the music also. She was in Manila when auditions happened the first time around. She was only eleven when the producers arrived—too young to audition. She stood on street corners singing then. Her parents collected money from the tourists visiting Manila Bay. A half hour of singing would garner enough food to feed her family that night.

The musical went onto become a big hit in London and New York. They needed more girls to play the lead. They went to the Philippines again. She was 14, still too young. She strengthened her voice by singing in school productions and singing in front of malls. The producers came again when she was 18, but by then, Bless wasn't in the Philippines, she was singing and dancing in Japan.

By the time she was twenty-three, she had moved to Los Angeles, renting a room from a cousin of a cousin. She read in Filipino newspapers that the musical was coming to Los Angeles and they needed a cast. Bless knew this would be her chance. Living in the States had always been a dream—Oh, to be an American girl! The price to visit the States was steep, more money than she could ever save working in the Philippines. She knew other singers who traveled Asia making a living, with Japan as the big jackpot.

When she read that auditions for the musical were happening in her adopted city, she believed dreams do come true in America

●

Bless stood in line, waiting to be seen. She had been standing there for an hour and a half. She looked at the men and women in line, some of whom looked like people she had known in the Philippines. She wanted to talk to them, speak to them in Tagalog.

When she was in Japan, she liked talking to the other Filipino performers in Tagalog. It relaxed her, made her feel less lonely. She was about to talk to two girls in line, ask them where they were from. Manila? Cebu? She overheard their conversation. Their English was distinctly American and Bless decided against talking to them.

She knew they would ask her where she was from or inquire about how long she'd been in America. She didn't want to deal with those questions. There were plenty of Filipino Americans in her neighborhood, many her age. Rather than speak to them, she'd rather converse with their parents who knew what it meant to come from the Philippines, knew the weather—hot!—and eat the food.

One of her most stable ways of earning an income was working as a food server at a restaurant on Temple Street. She stood behind a glass counter and served Filipino cuisine to customers. Most were families in the neighborhood or business people nearby. Every once and awhile, students from UCLA or USC came by to order food. They were studying Asian American studies or some such often touring Chinatown, Koreatown, Little Tokyo to taste authentic ethnic food.

Filipino students would come to Hi-Fi and order in their broken Tagalog. Bless thought it charming that they were trying to be as Filipino as possible. She would correct their enunciation occasionally. She watched them turn red.

"Don't be embarrassed," Bless said. "It's good that you're trying to learn Tagalog." Something Bless believed was that you couldn't truly be Filipino if you couldn't speak the language.

She watched these students eat, sturdy backpacks hanging on

their chairs. She'd stop by and offer to take away their plates and she'd hear them talk about a final exam, a football game, an essay. They always looked so clean and well mannered. These were the customers she preferred. She'd had it with drunken businessmen groping her, the way they did when she had entertained in Japan.

●

She stood in line for another hour waiting to audition. She had finally gotten into the waiting room. She looked around and saw posters for different musicals on the wall: A Chorus Line, 42nd Street, Chicago, Carousel. She sat back and couldn't believe that she was actually auditioning in a casting office in Los Angeles. Her neighbors couldn't believe it either. In addition to working at a restaurant, she also earned money singing at weddings, birthday parties, the dance club on Beverly Blvd. Wherever she worked, serving food or belting out a ballad, employers were familiar with her plight and paid her cash for her work. She sought out jobs that didn't require a social security number. Of course, living this way had its consequences. She sang at a birthday party, but her employer didn't want to pay her. She would leave despondent, but knew she had no recourse to collect her money.

In the casting office, she listened to girls enter the adjacent room and sing. They chose a pop song—a Whitney Houston ballad emanating from the closed doors—Bless chose to sing one of the songs from the actual musical. The BIG song that closes Act One. It spoke of wonder and despair, the future and the past converging. She knew it by heart because that was a song that she sang nightly in that bar in Tokyo.

She walked into the auditorium and handed her music to a pianist sitting nearby. Several people sat at a desk, their heads lowered. They were visibly tired. How many people could they have seen today? A hundred? Some yawned, some were making notes. She could swear that some were actually sleeping.

The pianist began to play her music, and she sang. All of them looked up, then leaned forward. She knew they would do this, suddenly become interested. In all of the bars where she'd sang, she'd had to deal with distracted audiences, from drunks to fighting couples. She learned to work to get their attention. Singing with emotion, dramatic gestures, a florid dress. She had learned how to take focus. This audition was no different.

She was asked back to meet with the producers.

●

At her callback, they asked her to sing again. They took her through the opening number, where she's introduced as a sweet village girl trying to make it in the big city. She nailed it. I'd been rehearsing that song since I was eleven, she thought.

"How long have you been singing?"

"Since I was little girl."

"Yes, it shows. It's a little rough."

"Your resume says you'd sung in Japan for several years, tell us about that."

It was the first time in this audition she felt queasy. On her resume, she'd listed productions that she'd acted in and theatres where she'd performed in Manila. For her four years in Japan, she simply wrote "touring."

"I sang in different night clubs." She couldn't tell them that they were hostess bars. She wore tight dresses and was paid to drink with businessmen after work. She made good money because there was a karaoke machine in the bar and she'd sing some choice love songs that made her more valuable than the other girls who simply sat there and looked pretty.

"Which places?"

"In Nagoya and Tokyo." She felt moisture building on her forehead. "But I'm so glad to be here in Los Angeles and auditioning for you. This has always been my dream."

"Let's have you sing some songs in the second act. By this time in the musical, our heroine is asked to do some unsavory acts, like engage in prostitution. I know it's difficult, but imagine having to do that when you sing this song."

"I'll try," she said. No problem, she thought.

"In this part of the show, you have to say good-bye to your son. Take it slowly. Imagine having to let go of someone you love."

Bless heard the few bars of the song, sad sounds coming from the piano. She closed her eyes and fell into the music. She didn't have a son to say farewell to, but she had other people. She thought of her parents and sisters, her little brother Manny who was going to be the first in their family to attend college. She thought of her cousins Dom, Alberto, and Susan who always believed in her talents as a singer. She remembered her dear childhood friend, Reza, who had recently gotten married. When she left, she told them that she looked forward to seeing them again. Something she thought would happen at the time. She didn't intend on becoming *tago ng tago*, TNT for short—or simply undocumented.

She sang all of her farewells into that song. When she was done, there was silence. She looked up and saw the men looking at her. She thought she had done something wrong. Until one, then two, then all of them started applauding.

"Bless, honey," the Director said, "can you wait outside? We have one other girl to see."

●

Bless sat in the waiting room and knew she'd done a good job. The door slowly opened and a pretty girl popped her head in. She had long, wavy hair and a great big smile.

"Is this the place?" the girl asked. "I'm here to audition."

Bless nodded.

"Oh, good," she said, "I got lost on the freeway, then got confused with the parking."

I took the bus, Bless thought.

"I'm Veronica."

Before Bless could introduce herself, Veronica pulled open a portfolio with three different shots of her. One was a close up of her face, another a full body shot dressed in a business suit, and the third a picture of her wearing glasses. They were shots showing her versatility as an actress.

"Hi, I'm Veronica."

"Yes, I know. You told me already."

"I'm sorry," she said laughing. "Just nervous. Always get nervous. Lord knows how many auditions I've gone on and I still get nervous."

"Oh, how long have you been doing this?"

"Since I was thirteen or so."

"Me, too," Bless said sitting up, inching toward this girl.

"Yeah, high school of the performing arts, then Julliard. But they never tell you in school how to get rid of nerves."

"No, they don't."

"I can't believe I'm auditioning for this show again."

"You've done this musical before?"

"I did the Canadian tour, but I was the understudy. I just finished the national tour of the King and I. I understudied Tuptim. Before that I toured with Flower Drum. I understudied Linda Low. Always the understudy, never the bride. How 'bout you?"

"I've done shows in Asia. I moved to the States a year ago. My name's Bless."

"Bless? What a cute name. Only Filipinos would name their child that."

Bless noticed how the girl threw back her hair and applied the reddest lipstick onto her lips. Bless couldn't help but notice that this girl was also lovely. Her skin was flawless and her brows perfectly plucked.

"How long have you been waiting?" Veronica asked.

"I sang already, but they asked me to stay."

"Oh, they must really like you."

Bless smiled.

"My auditions haven't been so great. I haven't booked anything in months. I'm here for pilot season, and I feel like I'm spinning my wheels."

"You want to be a pilot?"

Veronica looked at her quizzically, then burst into laughter. "Aren't you precious? No, I'm auditioning for television pilots. It's that time of year. I live in New York, but live in LA in February and March, hoping to land a series."

"Oh."

The door opened, and the casting director came out.

"Veronica!" the casting director said.

"Stewart, how are you?"

Bless noticed how Veronica ran toward Stewart and hugged him like an old friend.

"I'm good. You're as lovely as always!"

"You're being too kind."

"Are you ready?"

"Sure," Veronica said, entering the room. Bless took note of the round of hellos she got from the producers. They obviously knew her. Bless heard the music begin. Through the doors, she could hear Veronica sing—oh, such a gorgeous voice. Bless knew it was an expensive voice, one that came from years of instruction and classes. Bless had mostly learned to sing by imitating singers on the radio and countless attempts at karaoke.

Veronica was in there for a long time. She, like Bless, sang song after song from the show. Finally, Veronica emerged. She picked up her things and said, "Good luck, Caress. I have another audition in an hour, gotta run."

Bless continued to sit in the waiting area, wondering if Stewart and the producers had forgotten about her.

The door opened, and Stewart asked Bless into the room.

She stood on stage, looking at the men.

Stewart smiled, "We'd be honored if you sang the lead in our musical. Congratulations!"

●

Bless stuffed her last blouse into her luggage. She'd said her good-byes and arranged for a taxi to the airport. That had seemed so sophisticated to take a taxi to the airport. It would be a long plane ride, so she then went and ate her favorite meal in Los Angeles, a big, chili burger from Tommy's Hamburgers on Beverly Blvd. She would miss this!

She took a long walk around her neighborhood and would remember the names of its beautiful streets: Beverly, Coronado, Dillon, Vendome. She watched the children walk home from school. Such nice children. Besides the Filipino kids, she'd miss the Mexican and Korean children with baseball caps covering their faces.

A breeze suddenly swept across her face, and she exhaled. It was cool and friendly. She would miss this Los Angeles weather—this climate. She finally understood what Spring meant. It may have gotten hot, but nothing like the tropical heat of the Philippines.

She pulled out the producer's letter from her back pocket. She read it again. She'd read it a million times. She'd keep it with her, perhaps even frame it to show anyone who didn't believe her that she had actually been cast in the musical. How many girls can actually say that?

She would always love this city, this America. She could honestly say that she had lived in the States, something anyone from the Philippines would have given an arm for. She believed in opportunities, and liked to think she had taken them as they came along. Like the chance to come to America. She'd obtained a tourist visa, and planned to stay for a month, using the money she earned entertaining in Japan. But she loved the city and decided not to return. She'd lived in Los Angeles for 18 months before she auditioned for the musical. And it took less than two weeks to get the letter from the producers. She'd memorized its contents:

Dear Ms. Velasco,

We were thrilled to have you star in our musical. Your voice has a quality that we'd always associated with the lead role: innocent, strong, hopeful. We've seen many girls audition for this part, and we believe that your voice was one of the strongest we've heard.

However, Actors Equity informed us of your lack of documentation. If we had power over labor issues, we'd keep you right now. The state of immigration today is very touchy, and it wouldn't be wise to keep you in our show.

I suggest you go back to the Philippines, obtain the proper visas and try again.

Sincerely,
Steward Madeski.

Try again. Bless knew these words well, wondered if trying would be worth her time anymore. She would return to the Philippines, but didn't think she'd return to the States. She had known that going against the stipulations of her tourist visa was a big gamble. She'd heard stories of those who did that, and never got the leniency to return to America again. They might audition in the Philippines again, but she didn't know if she would audition. She had gotten the part already. She beat out a girl who'd sung the role already and been trained by the best in America and was even auditioning for pilots.

She folded the letter then returned to the house. She gathered her luggage, deciding to wait for the taxi out front. She began to hum. It was a melody she'd never heard before, a song she improvised in her head. It was an upbeat number, one that led her to smile.

A Letter Written at Tommy's Hamburgers

Dearest Pia,

After work, I eat at Tommy's Hamburgers on Rampart and Beverly. It is world famous in Los Angeles, but we have not heard about it in the Philippines. Tommy's is a small shack painted white and red—a Santa suit left on a corner of this city.

Filipino children run around here, looking like brown cotton balls pushed by wind. I am reminded of our Inday and Norbert Junior. Tell them I see them when my eyelids close.

Policemen and criminals, fancy people and the homeless eat chiliburgers against a wall, wiping away melted cheese from their lips. All are equal when the food is good and the price is cheap. Enclosed is some money that I know you will use wisely.

Sometimes, I work late. I still go to Tommy's. It is open 24 hours. Like my heart that awaits you.

Love,
Norby

Laconic Messages of Love

You'd sung the Kyrie at 9am, every Sunday morning for the past four years. You'd sung this hymn—one that asked God and Jesus for Mercy—well over 200 hundred times. It had lost meaning for you. This time, during this Mass, you want the words to mean something. Not because it was Thanksgiving mass and they *should* mean something. Not because hundreds of people were expected to attend. But because this would be the very last time you would sing the Kyrie with this choir.

The choir robe you were required to wear felt uncomfortable. The long, draping black garment was made of some kind of synthetic fabric, your body heat rose under the robe, forcing you to fan yourself with the missal whenever you could. You used the arm of the black robe to wipe away the sweat building at your temples. You couldn't wait for Mass to begin. You hoped that when you sang the Kyrie, you would mean every single word.

You had lifted the robe above your knees, letting cool air ride up your crotch. The worse thing about sitting up in the choir loft was that all the heat rose to you. Underneath your robe, you worried that the heat would dull the creases you meticulously ironed into your pant legs. You could feel the sweat staining your shirt, and you dreamed of services ending so you could discard the robe forever.

The robe never used to bother you. For the first year and a half, you enjoyed wearing it. It distinguished you from the rest of the churchgoers, letting everyone know that you were there to sing, to influence worship. For the first year and a half, you enjoyed the way the robe draped your slender body, bringing out your shoulders. You liked the blackness of the robe complimenting your hair, bringing the color out of your skin, matching the dark tortoise shell glasses that made your rather round face more oval.

You turned around to watch the faces of your fellow choir members—Filipino men and women who were at least a generation older than you. You softened your vision, making all of what you saw one huge blur. This was a habit you developed to kill time, taking away the definitions of their faces, creating a screen of melded color. What you saw on that screen was an earthen brown with a shimmering of orange. Every once in awhile, depending on how the sun hit the stained glass, the earthen brown was blessed with a purple or a red or a blue, reminding you of a toy kaleidoscope you had when you were nine.

You squeezed rosaries in your hand, enjoying the crunching sound they made. You enjoyed reciting the prayers of the rosary. You felt more comfortable praying to the Blessed Virgin Mary. Not because the church recognized her as the Queen of Heaven. Not because she watched her only son die. But you felt a woman in the Catholic church would better understand you. Indeed, most of your friends were women, had always been women.

You were quite good at reciting the prayers of the rosary which included fifty-three Hail Mary's, six Our Father's, six Glory Be's, and the Apostles Creed. The entire process lasted forty minutes. You were proud of the fact that you could do it all under five. In one breath you could squeeze out three Hail Mary's.

Your family wanted you to enter the seminary. They somehow knew you would never marry; priesthood was the only logical choice. The priesthood was an occupation every good Catholic boy had considered at one point or another, but earlier this year, when you experienced the pleasures of the flesh by being kissed by a man for the very first time, you knew the priesthood was not for you. It was that kiss that made you decide to leave the choir. It was that kiss that helped you see God.

You had always been an admirer of great Catholics. You were familiar with the lives of many saints, but it was the modern Catholics you followed the most. You clipped out stories from *People magazine* of Corazon Aquino, you still grieved the death of Mother Theresa, and you kept a picture of Pope John Paul on your bedroom wall. You were very happy to hear of Pope John Paul acknowledging gays in the church; it was okay to be homosexual, but it was a sin to engage in homosexual acts. So, when you went to the gay bars, as long as you didn't dance with a man, you wouldn't be sinning. Frankly, as much as you wanted to, you never danced at all.

You had been doing this since you had turned twenty-one, being gay, going to gay places, but careful not to engage in any gay behavior. You made it a point to dress and behave masculine. You kept your hair conservatively short. And, no matter how lonely you felt, no matter how your heart ached for companionship, you never touched another man unless it was a handshake.

Until a Stranger bumped into you in a bar in West Hollywood...

It was dark, and the Stranger mistook you for someone else. The Stranger uttered someone's name and gave you a hug. Your body recoiled into itself, and you made a quick mental prayer, noting that you are NOT hugging this man back—God, please know this is not a homosexual act.

The Stranger's hug was odd. It was not sexual, nor was it friendly. It was simply polite, barely touching him, but you were aware of the fact that you were being entirely enveloped.

The Stranger pulled away, and a strobe light had fixed itself onto your face, blinding you. You squinted trying to see, but the strobe light was harsh. You were able to see only when the Stranger tilted his head to the left intercepting the fierce white light. As you blinked trying to regain your vision, the strobe light had created a curious glow behind the Stranger's head.

You said, "You have the wrong person. I don't know you."

The Stranger said, "Maybe someday you will."

You had heard many pick-up lines before, and what this man said would have been one of those lines if it weren't for the way he said it. There wasn't a hint of seduction, a note of sexual foreplay in this line. The Stranger's voice was smooth. If velvet had a sound, this would certainly be it.

The Stranger lifted your hand. You saw your hand disappear into the blackness of the His silhouette. You felt the Stranger's lips rest on the knuckle connecting to the forefinger. A gentle kiss, rather motherly. The kind given to a sleeping baby.

In a kiss, in a club, with cigarette smoke rolling past like blue waves, music blaring, songs spewing laconic messages of love, people dancing to a confined claustrophobic space, you felt the presence of God: an overwhelming sense of calmness, a kind of relief, the perception that you would never be hurt and the belief that you would always be protected. For the first time in your life, you understood the meaning of the word: free.

As quickly as it came, the kiss was over. The moment was gone. And so was the Stranger, departing, disappearing into bobbing heads matching the beat of the music.

The following week you announced to your choir members that you would be leaving the choir. They threw you a small party. When one of the choir members asked you why you were leaving, you simply said, it was time to move on.

You didn't say what you truly felt. You didn't say that you had met God. Not in a church with an emaciated man on a cross. Not in a hymn centuries old. But in a smoky club where the men danced with each other.

For this very last time, sitting in the choir loft, you sang the Kyrie, which had all of three lines:

Lord, have mercy.

Christ, have mercy.

Lord, have mercy.

In the fleeting moments of Mass, you knew Mercy had been granted.

Acknowledgements

I must acknowledge my first writing teacher Ayofemi Folayan. She was a fierce, black lesbian poet who encouraged me to be unabashedly myself. May she rest in prose, poetry, and power.

Through workshops and various editors, I managed to get these short stories out in the world. I'll try to remember them all, but please forgive me if I should falter.

Thanks to my agent Al Zuckerman at Writers House. His guidance has been invaluable. Many thanks to the teachers, classmates, editors, and friends.

It took a lot of people to get these stories done. They include Patrick Ryan, Karen Sorenson, Leslie Schwartz, Hope Edelman, Carol Ojeda-Kimbrough, Claire Boyle, Nyol Lueth Tong, Eduardo Santiago, Meghan Daum, Bruce Bauman, Carlene Sobrino Bonnivier, Gerald G. Gubutan, Paul Lisicky, Amie M. Evans, Paul J. Willis, Peter Dubé, and Nita Noveno.

Much love to mom and my siblings Joy, John, and Jessie. Always appreciative of your support Mary Weatherford, William Weinberger, Brady Rubin, Philip Harrison, Jonathan Skurnik, and Jessiline Berry.

And, of course, Sven Davisson and the team at Rebel Satori. Seeing your "yes" in my inbox wishing to publish my manuscript brought about such incredible joy. I will be forever grateful.

9 781608 642809